Westward Wanderers

-BOOK ONE-

Where
He
Leads

Angela Castillo

To all who have wandered.

And the Voracious Reader.
I hope you like this one.

Author's Note

From the 1840's to the 1860's, the Oregon trail, a 2000-mile path unraveling between Missouri and Oregon, was a journey of choice for thousands of adventurous souls. What would drive folks to take such a dangerous trip?

Many were drawn in by the promise of free land, or the talk of fertile soil and rich harvests. Women and children were forced to go with urgent men or be left destitute. Truthfully, there were as many reasons to go as people who went.

I've attempted to spin a tale for one of these people. Though all characters and incidents are fictionalized, I've striven with all my heart to share as accurate a history as I could find. It's a curious study, of people with undeniable courage, unshakable faith, and unbelievable strength.

This book mentions Native American groups and the stigma that would have been associated with these people at this time. This has been written with all due respect for the cultures involved and the greatest attempt to be sensitive, but accurate.

A special thanks to Sarah Raymond Herndon, who lived it all and whose writings were a great inspiration for this book. You can find a wonderful recount of her tales in *Days on the Road: Crossing the Plains in 1865*.

I
Unexpected Meetings

Ami hurried down the street, weaving through people lost in their own Tuesday errands. A peddler held out a silver hand-mirror for her inspection, and a little girl reached out a chubby hand to stroke the shimmering fabric of her dress.

"Don't touch, Abigail!" A woman jerked the child's hand away. "The fine lady doesn't want her gown soiled."

"She's not a bother." Ami touched the little girl's crimson cheek. "I might have done the same thing at her age."

A carriage flew past, much faster than prudent in the crowded square. Ami jumped to the side to miss a spray of sand and pebbles. "Oaf driver," she murmured.

She made her way to the butcher's shop and hesitated in front of the battered door. The building was always stuffy, smelly, and buzzing with flies. "Oh, why did I promise Nancy I'd check for lamb chops?" But the dish was her own favorite, so she held her breath and cracked the door open.

Before Ami could step inside, she noticed a woman rushing down the street. The woman's dress, filled with countless petticoats and a hoopskirt, billowed around her, dragging through the mud with no heed.

Ami paused as she recognized Martha Davis. The woman wasn't one for fancy clothes, since her family was considerably poorer than the Kents and a mother with seven children rarely had the time or need for such deportment. Ami's curiosity was piqued even further when Martha pushed the cumbersome skirts to one side and plopped down on a hitching block a few yards away, narrowly preventing her crinoline from being exposed to the street. The middle-aged woman fanned her red face with the sheaf of papers in her hand.

Ami ran to her, curiosity burning in her soul almost as fiercely as concern. "Dear Mrs. Davis, whatever has brought you to this state?"

Martha sucked in a breath and smiled. "Oh, hello, Ami. I hope you are well. This corset is quite constricting. Gave up wearing them three children ago. I don't know how I managed to put it on, and I'm certainly unsure I'll ever get out of the garment."

"Oh dear," was all Ami could think to say.

"I'll be fine," Mrs. Davis waved her papers. "However, I've returned from a meeting. Tom felt it prudent to look as respectable as could be managed. I've been to the bank, you see."

"I see," said Ami, though she didn't. Martha Davis had been her mother's closest friend and confidant, but Ami mostly only nodded to them at church since her mother's passing two years ago. The Davis family had lived a quiet life with few scandals in their history, so they remained out of town gossip for the most part. That is, until Mr. Davis had up and left town the year before.

"It's Tom," Mrs. Davis continued, swinging her feet, like a little girl would do, so her thick leather shoes thudded against the wooden surface. "As you probably know, he took my two oldest boys to Oregon last May, they're twelve and fourteen. They've been building our home on our land. Forty acres we have and every inch of it free. I was meant to bring the rest of the children out next year."

Ami gasped. "How courageous of you."

"Courageous or addled," Martha rolled her eyes. "Tom's had to take on other work, trapping for pelts and the like, to pay for supplies and keep the boys' bellies full. Everything's more costly than we considered." She wiped a line of sweat from her forehead. "He's had to leave my boys alone for days at a time, and I don't like it. I've decided to go this spring instead of next year." She held out the top paper from her sheaf, and it shook in her fingers. "And here's the note from the bank."

Ami examined the bill of sale. "They bought your house?"

Mrs. Davis nodded. "The home belonged to my grandfather, so it's in my name. Wasn't a male heir." She sighed. "I wish I could have gone to Oregon when Tom went. But he left so soon after the war. Random Johnny Rebs still roaming. And me with a newborn babe in my arms." She tapped her chin. "Part of me hoped he'd change his mind and come trundling home. But he didn't. And if I ever want to see my boys again, I'll be braving the trail with my other children."

"Oh, Mrs. Davis." Ami struggled to find a comforting word, but imagination failed her.

"It's all right, dear." Mrs. Davis jumped down from the hitching block and gave her a bright smile. "Providence will see us through, sure as sure. I'm glad to have my Ellie. Seventeen and sharp as a tack, but since her bout with scarlet fever last year, she's been waning. It'll be a struggle to keep four little un's bobbing along the trail in a straight line. I'd like to hire a girl to come along." She examined the papers in her hands. "But who'd gallivant away to Oregon, off the top?"

"I'm sure I don't know, Mrs. Davis." Ami suddenly remembered her errand. She took the woman's hand, damp with sweat. "I will remember you in my prayers. Every day, not only Sunday."

"Thank you, dearie." Mrs. Davis squeezed her fingers. "Call on me if you have a chance. I always love to see those kind brown eyes, so much like your mother's."

As Ami left the butcher's shop with her parcel, drops of rain, round and ripe, hit her with such force that she wondered if Mr. Gootleg's twin boys were throwing rotten tomatoes again. But after the first few spotted her dress and bonnet brim, the droplets turned into a torrential downpour.

She darted under a nearby saloon's awning and clutched her reticule tighter. Tucked inside was a sample of the glorious magenta silk she'd commissioned for her ball gown. Silk was worth a fortune, and most of the women in town would give their eye-teeth for such a scrap. Ami was well aware of this, but these thoughts always brought a mixture of emotions. A swell of pride for her father, who worked his way up from a child of Dutch immigrants to one of Missouri's finest builders. And an imagined scolding from her mother, who had been raised in an impoverished pastor's family and taught her not to put on airs.

She brushed a tear from her cheek that had mixed with the rain. Though Mama had been buried and gone for two years now, certain memories still sent tiny pinpricks to her soul. During the funeral, the pastor had said Mama was looking down from a cloud with the angels, but Ami hated the thought of her being so far away. Too distant to see what went on in Ami's life, and too far to hear when she said a quick hello. Which might be scandalous. *Is speaking to a dead loved one blasphemous?* She'd long since stopped trying to ask Reverend Balder these questions. He was mortified by her forwardness and instead of answering, always assigned her memory verses that had nothing to do with the original inquiry.

Rain fell in sheets now, and she couldn't stay in front of the saloon. Anyone who saw her there would surely traipse off to Millany to report. Her stepmother had eyes and ears all over town.

My second-best bonnet shall be ruined. A dandy one, with bits of ostrich plume imported from Darkest Africa and snippets of ribbon from the upcoming ball gown. Dorothy Anne, her dressmaker and dearest friend, would be so upset.

As the rain relented for a moment, a yawning entryway across from the saloon beckoned to her. She hurried through the now ankle-deep rivulets of water that rushed down the street in miniature torrents.

At least she'd had the presence of mind to wear riding boots instead of her calling slippers. The more sensible footwear ushered her to safety, and she ducked into the cavernous building, unsure of her fortuitous sanctuary.

The rich scent of soaped leather and hay greeted her nose. Horses snorted greetings from a row of stalls.

The livery stable. Of course. Ami hiked up her bedraggled skirts and went to the closest steed.

"Hello there. Aren't you a beauty?" she crooned to a massive black stallion with a bright blaze across his muzzle. She scooped a handful of oats and lifted them up. The stallion picked each oat from her outstretched palm with velvety lips.

"Looks like General fancies you." A tall, slender man with a thick black mustache strode through the door. He tipped the edge of his bowler hat. "Good afternoon, ma'am."

Ami pressed her fingers against her shirt front. "Goodness, you gave me a start." Her hands flew to her bedraggled hat. "Pardon me. I slipped in to escape the deluge."

The man held out a gloved hand. "General and I are glad you did. Name's Paul Amos."

"Amethyst Kent. But everyone calls me Ami." Ami placed her hand in his, and Paul brushed it with a kiss.

A tingle ran down Ami's arm.

Paul let go of her hand and strode over to General. "Rain appears to be letting up. I'm planning to hitch General to my carriage," he gestured to a small buggy nearby. "I'm on my way out of town, but if you like, I could give you a ride home."

"That would be lovely." Ami's heart flip-flopped in her chest. *Would it be prudent to take a ride home from a stranger? He's obviously a gentleman.* She raised her chin. *I am nineteen, after all. I'm old enough to make up my own mind. And home's fifteen minutes away. Barely a wink and a nod until we get there.*

Paul smiled. "Bear with me, it takes a while to get him settled. There's a crate right there if you'd care to sit a spell." He waved a gloved hand at the mentioned item.

"Goodness no, I'll help you with the tack." Ami waltzed over to the buggy to check the shafts. "I spend a lot of time in my father's stables. Our groom, Ol' Pat, has taught me everything there is to know about horses. He says I could ride before I took my first step."

"Ah." Paul turned from the stall. "How does your husband feel about you spending your days riding?"

Ami let out a short laugh. "He'd be hard pressed to have a say in the matter, since he doesn't exist."

Paul arched one aristocratic eyebrow. "Yes, that would make it a bit difficult."

Ami leaned on a stand before her, resting her chin in her hands. "Mister's my best friend. He'd be lonely if I didn't spend time with him."

"Mister?" Paul darted her a slanted glance.

"My bay thoroughbred. Couple of hands smaller than General, but he's a beauty."

"I'm sure he is." Paul led General out of the stall and began running his palms down the massive, gleaming legs. "As you can see, I fixed the harness before finding my breakfast at the inn. I need to check him for swelling, we travelled a long way yesterday."

"Oh?" Ami felt it rude to ask for more information, though questions swam through her mind. Surely she'd have heard if someone from town was expecting a handsome gentleman visitor.

"Yes." Paul finished with the last leg and led the horse to the buggy's shafts. "Back up, boy. There's a good one."

The horse did as he was told as meekly as a Sunday school teacher. Ami smiled. *A pleasure to see a man who knows how to work with horses.*

She fastened the shaft on one side while Paul worked on the other. Captain tossed his mane and gave tiny whickers.

"That's it then." Paul came over to her side and gave a few tugs on the traces. "Snug as a bug. Let's get you home, Miss Kent."

She took his offered hand and sprang into the gleaming leather seat. That same tremor ran through her at his touch, even through their gloves.

"The trip home isn't long," she said, trying to keep the regret from her voice.

"At least the ride will save your skirts from further ruin." He gestured to her dress, where the mud and damp had already crept up the hem by several inches.

"Oh, yes. Thank you." Brenda, her personal maid, would be horrified as it was. But the shower truly had come out of a perfectly clear sky. It wasn't as though she'd meant to get soaked. Besides, these things always seemed to happen to her and Brenda was a dear soul who loved her no matter what.

As the buggy trundled into the street, a bit of chill air hit the wet spots on Ami's dress and she was tempted to scoot just a few inches closer to the handsome Paul Amos. But she shook her head. *You scandalous thing, you! Millany would be appalled.*

Not that it wouldn't be fun to see her father's second wife's shocked expression. *She'll already be mad about me ruining my clothes. Better not throw fuel into the fire.* Most of her encounters with Millany in the last few weeks had been fraught with tight-lipped tension on both sides. It was a good thing Amy would be going to Sasha Regent's coming out ball in a month. *We need a rest from each other.*

Paul rubbed the back of his neck. "I just realized you haven't told me where you live,"

"Oh, goodness, how silly of me! You're headed in the right direction. I live south of town, on Granbury Street."

"You'll have to direct me." Paul settled back in his seat. "I'm new to these parts. Passing through, really."

"Oh?" Ami tried to emphasize the question a bit, hoping he would take the hint.

"Yes." He rested his elbow lazily on the back of the buggy seat.

She held her breath, wondering if he'd be so forward as to put his arm around her, but he didn't.

"I'm heading to Independence. I intend to sell my buggy and join an outfit for Oregon."

"Oh." The little castles in the air Ami had begun to build came crashing down in heaps of rubble. Oregon was a lifetime away. And unless you counted teamsters and scouts, the folks who went down that trail never came back. "You're the second person today to tell me they've decided on that particular venture."

"There's fortunes to be had and land to be settled," Paul said. He adjusted the reins that he'd wrapped around his whip. "And it's our God-given duty to claim the land with civilized boots, wouldn't you say?"

Ami stared down at Paul's meticulously polished boots and tried to imagine him as a settler of new lands, but the idea didn't quite measure up. She murmured something in assent and then became quiet for the rest of the trip, only answering yes or no to Paul's cheerful babble or pointing out the correct direction when they reached a fork in the road. By the time her father's stately home and grounds appeared over the horizon, the sun streamed over the front lawn, and raindrops sparkled on bright April grass.

"This is my home." She waved her hand towards the gate.

He stopped the buggy on the drive, came around and helped her step down. "Mind the mud, it's still thick here," he said.

"Thank you for the ride, Mr. Amos." Ami shook his hand. "Be careful on your trip."

"Course I will," said Paul. "If you're ever in Oregon, you could come and ride with me again."

Ami couldn't help but chuckle at the absurdity of his statement. "I'll do that," she replied. An invitation to luncheon rested on her lips, but she'd already been too forward, too brazen, by accepting a ride in the first place.

With nothing more to say but "Goodbye and thank you," Ami uttered both phrases in haste and trudged down the sodden drive to the courtyard, her voluminous skirts growing heavier by the step.

###

As Ami rushed in, she passed Millany.

The tall, stately woman pressed her hand on a pane of glass in the drawing room window that ran from floor to ceiling. No other home in Memphis had a window so large, with four-and-twenty sections and the top four made of red colored glass. Mama had loved the window, but Ami had always felt a bit afraid of the room because in the morning sun, the light shining through the top panes seemed to her like blood streaming over the white pine floor.

Millany wore her house dress, a green taffeta, which was only slightly less grand than the dresses she chose for calling. It rustled like leaves in the fall as she turned to face Ami, looking for all the world like an exotic plant, her titian hair dressed in a flaming pompadour at the top.

Her pale cheeks reddened. "Amethyst Kent! Where have you been? And what happened to your dress?"

Ami bit her lip, ruing her decision to enter through the front and not the servant's door. She wasn't afraid of her stepmother. After all, Millany had been her school mate and only four forms ahead. At eight years of age Ami had whipped her in a fight when Millany had mocked her for spelling 'miscreant' incorrectly. Ever since then, the two had been at odds and Millany's introduction to the Kent household had only worsened the problem.

Millany did everything she could to make Ami's life miserable, but when Ami's father was home she played the victim, creating elaborate descriptions of the wrongs Ami had committed. Father often berated Ami, despite her protests, and then left the scene, commanding the 'women work out their differences."

This evening, Ami simply didn't wish to endure any sort of conflict after the heartsick disappointment she'd experienced mere moments before. *And I WILL be heartsick,* she answered her own admonishment. Paul Amos was as goodly as any eligible man she'd met in Memphis, and there were precious few of those in the first place. *Why didn't I invite him to lunch?*

"You look a fright." Millany's voice shook. "Your father's perfectly good money poured into a dress and you've ruined it. And furthermore," she turned, her hands clenched at her sides, "I can't believe you'd allow yourself to be seen in that state. What will my friends say?"

Ami rolled her eyes. Her stepmother's focus in life was looks, fashion, and what everyone else thought. She didn't care what had to be done or who must be hurt to get what she wanted, in any situation.

"I was caught in the sudden shower, Millany. I didn't intend to ruin my dress today, but you have nothing to fret over. I'm fairly sure your friends all stayed in their homes to prevent their sugar-spun souls from melting."

Millany turned back to her brooding stance at the window, her lips in a tight line.

Though she spoke not a word, Ami knew what she was thinking, for she'd overheard Millany say it to a friend. "The girl is common, as her mother was common, for all her father's wealth. Can't make a silk purse from a sow's ear."

Ami shook away the irritation she always felt when she remembered that conversation. No matter how hard she tried, she'd never be good enough for her stepmother. She was weary of the attempt.

Millany snapped her head back as quick as a rattlesnake. "I'm vexed with you. Leave my sight."

Biting back a flood of angry words, Ami rushed up the stairs as fast as she was able.

As Ami reached her room she rang a little servant's bell. She'd barely had time to undress before Brenda's familiar plodding steps approached her door.

The maid popped her head in. "Will you be needing a bath drawn then, Miss Ami?"

"Yes, please, Brenda." Ami gestured to a pile of sodden clothing bundled on a chair. "And I'm afraid my clothes are a mess. I got caught in the sudden shower today."

"Your best dimity." Brenda shook her head until her lace cap rustled. "This is going to take a sight of washing, and I'm not sure I'll ever be able to get the train back to snowy again."

"I know, and I'm sorry." Ami perched on the low-lying window seat in her chemise and bloomers. "I don't know what possessed me to ask for a train in that color. Dorothy Anne raised an eyebrow, but she didn't say anything. I wish she'd warned me."

"Probably worried you'd throw one of those rich folks temper tantrums." Brenda chuckled.

Ami's mouth fell open. "Brenda, I would never."

Brenda picked up Ami's muddy boots and placed them outside her door. "No, your mother wouldn't have stood for it. She raised you right, your mother did. She wasn't nothing like Mrs. Fancy Missy out there."

Ami folded her arms tight over her chest. She and Brenda moaned about their common dislike for Millany often. The tension that arose between stepmother and stepdaughter was stifling, and Ami often placated Millany's ridiculous demands simply to keep the peace. *Mother wouldn't have wanted us to live in a house of strife.*

###

That night, Ami blew out her lamps and snuggled down under her feather coverlet. Thoughts of Paul rose over all others in her mind. His confident smile. His infectious laugh. He was the kind of man who'd have women hanging on to his every word at a dinner party.

He's going to Oregon, she kept telling herself. *He'll probably die of dysentery anyway, or get gut-shot by a raider.*

But she stayed awake far longer than she'd ever admit to a living soul, dreaming of a handsome man in a bowler hat.

2
An Unfortunate Dinner

Ami's father's voice boomed through the rear foyer. "Heading out to the stables so early, Amethyst?"

Ami stopped with a hand on the door's latch. Her heart thudded against her chest. "Goodness, Father, you gave me a fright. Yes, I planned to ride this morning, since the weather is so much nicer than yesterday. I didn't think you'd object."

Mr. Kent crossed his arms over the front of his smart black waistcoat. His walrus mustache twitched. "Millany said you haven't been helping with household duties. You must complete indoor tasks before gallivanting off on your horse."

"Duties?" Ami gave a short laugh. "Are you referring to the morning drill where Millany lines up the servants in the drawing room to pour shortcomings over their heads? No, I'm not interested in being a part of that little ritual, thank you."

A small vein popped out on her father's bald forehead. Ami watched in fascination as it bulged larger and larger while he spoke. "Amethyst Kent, you promised to do your best to keep the house running smoothly after your mother's passing. I expect you to keep your word. Servants must be tended to, or everything will go to the dogs. You know this."

Ami took her father's hand. "Father, we have five servants in the home. Five. Three of them have been with us since I was a baby. They could run the house by themselves, even if we went abroad for a year and left them to their own devices. We're hardly approaching chaos."

Father shook away her hand, a gesture he would have never done two years hence. Turning from her, he studied an oil painting of chrysanthemums hanging on the wall that Ami's mother had painted years ago.

Ami was surprised Millany allowed the painting to remain in sight. *Probably still trying to come up with an excuse to take it down.*

Ami's father clenched his fist and drew it under his chin. "You women are going to pull me to pieces. I can't abide this constant fiddle-faddle much longer. It's not good for my constitution."

A wild hope rose in Ami's heart. Would Father send Millany away? Divorce wasn't unheard of, but it was mostly reserved for wives who had gone mad or been glaringly unfaithful. Of course

Millany hadn't done anything so reprehensible. A lump of guilt rose in her throat. *How could I think such a thing? Father would never be so cruel.* And as much as she hated to think it, he would never choose Ami's side. *Not now.*

Mr. Kent pulled a kerchief from his breast pocket and polished the head of his ever-present silver-knobbed walking cane. "Amethyst, you've always been a strong-willed child, but the generous nature inherited from your mother usually wins in the end. I'm calling upon that generosity of spirit in the request I'm about to make."

Ami swiveled to face her father, eyes darting over his features to check for signs of his intentions. The last time they'd had a conversation of this nature was the day her world ended, the day he'd informed her of his upcoming wedding to Millany. "Father, what would you ask of me?" Her voice rasped, sounding like an old woman's. Suddenly she wished very much for a glass of water.

"Sasha Regent. You're travelling to her coming-out party next month. The one you've been preparing all the frippery for." Mr. Kent raised a graying eyebrow.

"Yes, Father. It's the first party I'll be attending since Mother died."

Her father nodded. "Your mother's death was untimely for us all. I'm afraid it was most unfortunate for you, since that and the war prevented you from having your own coming out. I'm sorry your life has been suspended, as it were. Society suggests you should be married by now."

"I don't care what society says!" Ami burst out.

Mr. Kent waved a black-gloved hand. "No matter. I met with Bernard Regent, Sasha's brother, while on business in Springfield last week. You've met him a few times over the years. He works for the family company."

Bernard Regent? She'd avoided him at any cost. If it wasn't for Sasha absolutely begging for Ami's presence at the party, she wouldn't have agreed to go there, either.

Ami's father paid no attention to the pained expression that most assuredly had overtaken her features. He continued, an uncharacteristic grin spreading across his face. "Yesterday, Bernard asked for the honor of your hand."

"My . . . hand?" Ami stammered. "For what? Marriage?" She staggered back a step or two, then lighted on a waist-high column. Resting her hands on the rough stone, she closed her eyes, then opened them, hoping her father might have disappeared, that it would all be a dream.

"Of course in marriage, what else would it be?" said Mr. Kent. "He'd planned to broach the subject long ago, but after your mother's passing . . . "

"Threw a wrench into his plans, I suppose." Seething anger simmered in Ami's belly, and she clamped her jaws shut to keep it from spewing forth like an unquieted geyser. "You figured I'd be anxious to go along with a plan the two of you concocted," she managed to hiss. "Just like that."

Her father rubbed his chin. "Naturally, Bernard will ask you himself. After the coming-out ball so as not to overshadow his sister's celebration. I felt it prudent to inform you of his intentions ahead of time. These matters of matrimony take such thought and care, though I'm sure I don't know why." He brightened. "Perhaps you and Millany could arrange everything together, maybe that would help to iron out your troubles. Millany so loves to plan parties."

Ami clutched at the rough fabric of her riding habit and took deep breaths, trying to regain control. Her father had not been himself for so long. He'd quenched his grief too quickly by marrying Millany before it was hardly decent. His judgement could scarcely be trusted in matters of this nature.

Tell him, Ami. Tell him you found someone you could actually picture spending your life with, and that man will never be Bernard Regent. She bowed her head as she remembered. *Paul Amos is heading for Oregon. He might as well be dead.*

"Coming for dinner next week . . ." Her father's voice snapped her back into the moment. "Please consider his proposal, Ami. He's a fine man, with wonderful prospects."

A memory hammered at Ami's mind with driving force. Bernard Regent at a gathering years before, an ice cream social if she remembered right. He'd teased Carl Luxenburg, a crippled child, then taken his beloved toy boat and broken it to bits. And

Bernard had been fifteen, old enough to know the difference between right and wrong. After that, tales had run up the gossip chain to her ears. Bernard burning the wagon of a peddler who refused to move out of his way fast enough. Always using his father's money to cover his wrongs. An indiscretion with a barmaid. *But no one could prove that one.*

Each of these reasons were enough to convince her own heart, but her father would excuse them away as boyish follies. Ami decided on a different approach. "Father, I'm not interested in marriage at this time. I've told you, I don't love anyone, especially Bernard Regent."

Her father's face sagged, and he covered his eyes with a trembling hand. "I only want you to be happy and cared for," he murmured. "I'm doing the best I can for you. Give Bernard a chance."

Ami's resolve cracked into a thousand pieces, and she rested her hand on his arm. "I'll try, Father. I promise I'll try."

"Go away with you." Her father gestured to the door. "After you've had your ride, you must return and help Millany for the rest of the morning. We don't want her having another case of the vapors, do we?"

As Ami hurried to the stables, the freshly sprung compassion for her father began to dissipate and her anger twisted into a rage. *How dare he suggest I marry a man I care nothing for. He wants me out of the way, that's as clear as air. This was my home far longer than it's been Millany's! She's the stranger. How can*

Father choose her over me? By the time she'd stormed Ol' Pat without so much as a good morning, and saddled Mister, hot tears began to smart the corners of her eyes. On the ride down the road to the woods, they slid down her cheeks.

She scrubbed them away. *I'll look a fright by the time I pass the Martell house, and won't Vivien Martell crow if she sees me.*

Ami didn't truly care what Vivien Martell thought, except she was one of Millany's frequent callers, and she didn't want Millany to know she was upset. Ami refused to give her the satisfaction.

###

The dining room shone with brass. Brass candlesticks, brass fixtures, and the brass chandelier that hung over the dining room table. As always, candles flickered from the chandelier, which the servants brought down by means of a pulley system to light before dinner every evening.

The Kents never ate lunch in the dining room. That was what the breakfast nook was for. And breakfast was eaten in one's own room, at one's own small table in the corner, brought up by a servant. Dinner, without exception, was to be eaten in the dining room.

Ami pricked a morsel of lamb with her polished silver fork. Disapproval hung in the air like a monk's cowl, drifting from Millany's hunched shoulders and her father's frown.

Bernard Regent, unperturbed by the unpleasant atmosphere, stabbed a sizable chunk of his lamb chop and appraised it with a large smile that reddened his rosy cheeks even more than usual.

"A fine rack of lamb, Mrs. Kent." He balanced the food on his fork and folded it into thick meaty lips.

Staring was a sin second only to swearing, but Ami, morbidly fascinated, found it hard to pull her eyes away. Forcing her attention to her own plate of food, she found her appetite diminishing with every satisfied smack of Bernard's lips.

"I'm glad you find it to your liking, Mr. Regent." Millany patted her mouth with a dainty lace napkin. She wore a simple dark blue delaine and a strand of pearls around her snowy throat. Her red hair, arranged within an inch of its life, shone fiercely in the candlelight. A quick smile passed over her face, one that didn't reach the corners of her mouth.

Sasha Regent scooped a tiny spoonful of butter from the dish and placed it on her plate. "Dear Ami, Mrs. Kent said your dressmaker has been commissioning a new wardrobe?" A hopeful gleam filled her soulful eyes. Sasha Regent possessed the unfortunate luck of appearing as though she were forty, even though she hadn't reached her eighteenth birthday. A double chin was already developing, and her complexion was sallow. Her eyes sunk deep into her face as though they were too heavy for her flesh to support.

"Yes, she has." Ami swallowed a bite of potato, but the starchy substance stuck in her throat on the way down.

Sasha and Bernard gazed at Ami with expectant smiles, as though they hoped she'd say more, but Ami took a large swallow from the glass of water in front of her. The potatoes finally found their way down Ami's throat. "I have no more to say," she finally choked out.

Millany's glare would have scorched an ice block.

Mama would be scandalized at my rudeness. Ami tipped her head. *Mama would never insist I marry someone I didn't love.*

Bernard cleared his throat. "Mr. Kent, my father wanted me to pass along his thanks for the fine set of building plans you produced for the new Mercantile. The supplies cost substantially less, and the place is strong as Fort Knox. We could use it as a shelter for the next war." He frowned. "Not that there will be another war. My apologies for suggesting such a terrible thing."

"No apology needed." Ami's father waved his hand. "I'm pleased to hear the plans are to his liking."

Ami pulled her napkin from her lap and placed it over her barely touched meal. "May I be excused, Father? I'm feeling a bit unwell this evening."

Her father's eyebrows drew down over his nose as though she were a puzzle on a sheet of building plans. "Must you leave our guests?"

"I must." She stood swiftly and untangled her ridiculous skirt from the chair. She gave Sasha what she hoped was a sympathetic look, because she was the only person she truly felt apologetic to. "Please accept my regrets."

"Of course," Sasha murmured, blinking rapidly.

Bernard brushed her arm with his flabby fingers as she passed his chair. "Miss Kent, I'd hoped to ask you to join me for an evening stroll. Along with my sister, of course."

"My apologies, Mr. Regent, but I truly am ill," Ami replied through a tightened jaw. "I'm sure we'll have plenty of time to exchange pleasantries during Sasha's ball."

"Of course, Miss Kent." Bernard beamed, his jagged teeth catching the glint from a candle. "I look forward to it with great anticipation."

I'm sure you do. Ami stalked out of the room, taking care not to let her skirts catch on an ill-placed curio shelf near the dining room entrance.

She'd made it down the hall and had her foot on the first stair when she heard the unmistakable swish of Millany's dress over the wooden floor.

Ami considered dashing up the steps, but her dress might tangle around her ankles and cause her to plummet to her death. And if she didn't make it all the way upstairs when Millany minced into the hallway, she'd most certainly be ordered to come back down. She sighed and slouched against the bannister in a most unladylike way.

Millany's eyes glowed like embers in an angry fire. "Of all the things . . ." she hissed, wringing her laced-gloved hands. "Of all the things you've ever done, this is the worst. I worked my fingers to the bone to prepare a meal and the house for our guests, and this is how you serve me."

Ami bit back a short laugh. Millany had spent all afternoon in her sitting room with a glass of lemonade and Godey's Lady's Book. The only effort she'd put into this evening's meal was to tell Nancy, the cook, that she'd wanted lamb instead of veal. The servants had worked all day washing the already sparkling windows and woodwork, and Ami, herself, had dusted the pianoforte.

But none of these arguments would thaw Millany's frosty demeanor, so Ami answered, "My head is aching fearfully. I believe it's the sudden heat. Please apologize again to our guests."

As Ami turned on her heel, Millany caught her wrist. Her fingernails raked Ami's satin sleeve, leaving snags in the forest green fabric. "You think you're in control, miss queen of the manor. But you will marry Bernard Regent."

Ami couldn't keep her mouth from dropping open. "And what if I don't consent?"

"You'll wish you did." Two bright spots appeared on Millany's white cheeks. "I'll sell Mister." She dug her nails in a fraction deeper. "And you'd better believe your father will go along with it. You know whose side he's on."

Sobs caught in Ami's throat as she stumbled up the stairs in a haze. *How could she be so hateful?* She went into her room and closed the door. A drumming had intensified behind her temples during dinner; she hadn't lied about feeling ill. She sank down in the chair beside her vanity. After moistening a handkerchief in her water basin, she dabbed her forehead. *Sell Mister? Would Millany be that evil? Could she be?*

Ami rose, her head swimming. *Blasted corset.* Brenda had fastened the laces too tight.

Stumbling to her writing desk, she pulled out two sheets of paper, two envelopes, and a quill pen.

She wrote feverishly, the plan forming itself as pen flowed across paper.

When she was finished, she glanced outside. *Still light enough for Ol' Pat to make it to town and back.*

She rang the little bell and fanned the envelopes, willing the ink to dry. Her throat tightened as she considered the wheels she'd be putting into motion. *No one tells Amethyst Kent how to live her life. If they're going to try, then I won't be here for them to control.*

3

Secret Dresses

Dorothy Anne, Ami's dressmaker and best friend, shoved another pin into a hemline and frowned. The morning was young, with watery sunlight streaming through the windows of the tiny shop.

"I can see why you'd be upset, but don't you think this plan is extreme? For one thing, I'll never see you again. How will I make a living?"

Ami sighed. Humor was Dorothy's way of covering when she was upset. "Silly goose, you're the most popular dressmaker for miles. Kitty Blanchett will be thrilled to have you to herself."

Dorothy Anne wrinkled her nose. "Kitty Blanchett? I'm not sure the First Lady's dressmaker would be good enough for her." She shook out the garment she'd been working on. "One riding habit of brown denim, and I have two others packed away."

The dress was plainer than anything Ami had ever worn, but Dorothy had managed to add in a few frills here and there, and the collar was made from antique lace.

Ami examined the hemline. "No weights for the skirt?"

"I've read newspaper stories about the trail," said Dorothy Anne. "You won't want anything dragging you down. Which reminds me, I wouldn't suggest a corset, either."

Ami gasped. "No corset? Is that decent?"

Dorothy Anne shrugged. "Decency isn't always the best choice. A woman was telling me her sister was stabbed by a whalebone from her corset whilst out on the trail. The wound caught the gangrene and she died in her wagon." She pursed her lips. "Ami, are you sure about this? What are you going to do when you reach the end of the trail?"

Ami tapped her chin. "I've thought about that. Teach, maybe. Or I could become a seamstress, like you."

Dorothy Anne smiled. "I've seen your embroidery projects at school. Maybe something besides dressmaking."

Ami picked up a scrap of velvet ribbon and stroked it between her thumb and forefinger. "I hear there's plenty of rich folks in Oregon. I'm sure they need housekeepers. Goodness knows with Millany as a stepmother I've learned to do that." She glanced over at Dorothy Anne. "Don't worry. I'll manage to find a way."

"I know." Dorothy fiddled with the end of her dark brown braid. "It just seems like you're risking so much. Indian raids, wild animals, rattlesnakes." She scooted her chair back. "That reminds me. These came in yesterday." Pulling a box from under the shelf, she opened it. Inside were two pairs of sturdy leather shoes.

"They're horrid." Ami giggled. She stuck out her foot. "But much more useful and practical than these French kid shoes. I'm not attending a grand ball, after all."

She glanced at the magnificent dress Dorothy had hung up in the shop window in case Millany decided to come snooping around. Silk brocade in a deep maroon, the exact color to set off her perfect complexion and snapping brown eyes. The flounces and ruffles were too numerous to count, and the skirt was so wide she'd have to enter the doors sideways. A black silk hat with the smallest peep of a peacock's feather finished it off.

"You'd be the belle of the ball," Dorothy put her hand on her hip. "But instead you choose to waste my finest creation and wear clogging togs in the wilderness."

"Instead of a lifetime with an odious man." Ami sat on the padded chair opposite from the dressmaking table. "I'll take the togs, thank you."

"Oh, let's not forget your crowning glory." Dorothy pulled three giant calico monstrosities from beneath the counter. One was peach and purple, the other two were black and green. "I chose the prettiest colors I could find, but still."

Ami went into a of laughter. "Can you see me bobbing along the trail in those bonnets? I'll be like a horse with blinders! But they'll keep my skin from burning." She sobered. "Good thing Mister is sure-footed."

Dorothy Anne dropped the bonnets and gave Ami a tight hug. "Oh, my friend, will you truly be leaving in only three days? I'll never see you again."

Ami gripped her friend's hands. "You understand why I must go, don't you? Please say you understand."

"Yes." Dorothy folded the bonnets and put them away. "I couldn't be so brave, but I realize why you are making this choice.

I'm so fortunate to have my Frederick for a beau. He and Father are on such agreeable terms that Father asks me about wedding plans every day, the old dear. I can't imagine how I would feel if I felt forced to marry someone I loathed."

"Ol' Pat will be here to fetch my things tomorrow," said Ami. "I dare not take them home today, since Millany might see them and wonder why I'd need giant sunbonnets for a grand ball."

Trepidation filled Ami's heart as she finished packing the things remaining in her room. The three trunks in front of her were to be loaded in the coach, but she wouldn't be taking any of them to Oregon. These would be decoys to fool her father and Millany. The two smaller trunks filled with commissioned clothing and a few of her smuggled treasures were stowed away in Dorothy Anne's shop. Martha would take these with her family's coaches.

Ami circled slowly, surveying the space. The comfortable bed would soon be replaced by a straw tick or a thin blanket, infested by fleas or worse. A silver hairbrush and mirror set belonging to her grandmother were packed into the small valise that she'd carry with her, and fifty dollars life savings she'd squirreled away hung from a pouch around her neck. Thank God she'd never put it in the bank like her father had always urged. She'd have required to get his signature to withdraw it, and even if she hadn't, word would have surely spread around town that she'd pulled it out.

Her mother's gentle amber eyes watched her from the oval portrait over her bed. Magenta Kent had been the kindest, most wonderful person in the world. She'd invited hobos and orphans to eat at the family table and cried when they told their stories. More than one widow in town had a job because of her quiet recommendation.

Ami returned her mother's gaze. "Oh, Mother, I wonder if you'd approve! No, of course you wouldn't." She clutched at the mounded counterpane on her rumpled bed. "If you were still here, I'd have no reason to leave. You'd have set things right ages ago."

Her mother's words, said to her many, many times, came back to her mind. "Ami, my love, what would God have you do?"

That's the problem. I can't hear His voice in this matter. Though I've prayed a dozen times. I don't know.

Ami sat on her window seat and cranked a lever to open the windowpane. A rush of cool morning breeze fanned her face and freed the hair that had stuck to her skin. She closed her eyes. "It's a bit late to change my mind, God, but I'm listening. Please show me where to go."

She remained motionless for what seemed like hours.

Finally, a tiny ember of peace glowed in her heart. The warmth spread throughout her being, filling her soul with joy. A still, small voice spoke inside of her, and yet outside and all around, at once. "My child, I will lead you."

Ami crept through the darkened house, feeling every bit like a cat burglar. This wasn't the first time she'd stolen out for an early morning ride, and she knew where to avoid the squeaky places on each of the back stairs.

Lantern light glimmered in the stable window, and she slipped inside.

Mister shook his mane and stretched his beautiful head towards her, snorting.

Ol' Pat checked a stirrup and turned, tears streaming down his leathery face. He pulled a spotted handkerchief from the recesses of his coveralls and blew his nose loudly.

"That ol' battle-axe should never have threatened your horse," he wheezed. "Forcin' you to head out into a god-forsaken land by your lonesome. I shouldn't allow it."

Ami's blood froze, and she stood stock-still. She caught a tiny reflection of her white face in Mister's polished bridle. "Please, Ol' Pat. Please don't tell anyone." She'd had to recruit the old groom to deliver her messages and trunks. But she trusted him above all others. She hadn't dared to tell even Brenda her secret.

The firm wrinkled mouth softened and he patted her shoulder with a gnarled hand. "Don't you worry. I love you like my own, you know that. Ol' Pat vowed silence, and I'll take your secret to my grave, even if I'm fired for it. Didn't I teach you how to ride? Didn't I set up jumps for you out in the woods though your father forbade it? I could never say no to you, even when you were a bitty thing."

"I never considered that you could be fired." Ami rested her chin on her hands, pure misery hitting her like a thundercloud. "I've tried to cover my tracks, Ol' Pat. It should appear as though I've worked on my own."

"Don't you worry about me, Missy." Ol' Pat went to the barn entrance and gazed out over the field, where dots of color advertised the wildflowers just beginning to make their appearance for spring. "Breaks my heart to see you go away anywhere, but I know t'would kill you dead to give up that horse and marry that Regent boy. Better to traipse off into the wild with good people than marry into misery. My Ma married an awful man." His watery eyes drooped at the corners. "I wouldn't wish that on another soul in this world."

He cupped his palms beneath a stirrup, and though Ami hadn't needed help mounting in years, she lightly stepped in his hands and sprang into the saddle.

Bending down, she kissed his forehead. "I'll write you from Oregon," she whispered. "I owe you everything, Ol' Pat. Don't forget me."

Ol' Pat gave a wavering smile. "Honey, that would be like forgetting the sun in the sky."

###

Wind whipped into Ami's face, causing her eyes to smart with tears that sometimes blinded her. Not that she could see very well in the semi-darkness anyway. Thankfully she'd grabbed her thickest shawl, one that had belonged to her mother, to wind around her head and shoulders. She hunched over Mister's neck and prayed that no one she knew would be out this early in the morning.

With any luck her father would believe the hasty note she'd scribbled about taking the early coach to the Regent's home instead of the one departing at noon. And hopefully no one would think to check with the boarding house she was scheduled to stay at this evening. She'd already telegraphed them not to expect her the day before.

She could see them now; Millany's disapproving glare, and her father's irritated scowl. Her father would stomp and rage that she hadn't the propriety to say goodbye. Millany would worry about what her friends would think; that her own stepdaughter would step off to a party without the decency of a chaperone. Bubbles of guilt rose up in her heart, but she popped them with pins of practicality. *I wouldn't have gone If they hadn't driven me to it. Millany was going to take Mister.* This became a phrase repeated over and over, that drove her ever forward, and ever faster.

Dawn's rosy fingers quickly crept up the sky, lighting the old wooden bridge that spanned the river. Riding alone for such a distance was scandalous for a woman of her station, but she'd be facing much greater improprieties soon, from what she'd learned of the trail.

She passed a farm wagon, loaded with bales of hay. The driver gawked at her unabashedly as she passed. *No one I know. Thank goodness.*

Martha had told her the small town where the wagon train would be congregating was less than an hour's ride, but it seemed a lifetime before the trees began to thin out, and she knew she'd arrived.

4

Sacrifices

Shiloh Talon swung the last crate of dry goods over the wagon's edge and brushed his hands together. Tight fit, but the food would be eaten soon enough, and the crates used for precious firewood.

The second scout, Joe Loggins, sauntered up and crossed his arms. "That's all for it, then? Guess we'd better set up the mules."

"Guess we'd better." Shiloh sighed. He'd have thought twice before agreeing to scout this journey if he'd known they'd be running mules. Yes, mules were faster than oxen, but that didn't matter when most of a group had oxen and they had to keep in stride. Besides their well-known stubbornness, mules needed more rest, better feed, and had less stamina. He hated to no end when a wagon master was deceptive, gave him a bad taste in his mouth, but there would be no changing things now.

He glanced beneath the wagon and gave a low whistle. His dog, Shadow, bounded out from the cavernous depths, his ears bouncing with every hop.

"Shadow, you addled creature. Are you a dog or a Jack rabbit?" He scratched Shadow's head and the dog looked up at him, tongue lolling.

It was hard to believe that just sixteen months before, they had been side by side in a battle, left in a field of corpses. Compared to that, the four wagon runs he'd done seemed trivial.

Joe grinned at him. "You really take that mutt everywhere?"

Shiloh shrugged. "Man's best friend. You should see him hunt. Points out my game."

"That mongrel?" Joe chuckled. "I'd have to see it to believe it."

"Gets useful when you're hunting right before wagon call and don't have much time to get back to a train." Shiloh decided not to mention what happened on his first journey to California, before the war. He'd been a mere boy of nineteen when they'd crossed the mountains. Shadow had led him through a blizzard back to camp. Brought him mice and rabbits when they were holed up for a week in a cave. One of the many times the dog, with help from the hand of the Almighty, had saved his life.

"Hey, I forgot to tell you, I need to run to town before . . ." Shiloh's voice trailed off as he glanced at Joe's face.

His travelling partner stood stock-still, his eyes bulging out. "Will you look at her?" Joe whispered.

A woman approached the wagon train on a magnificent steed, her carriage suggesting years of experience in the saddle. She rode astride, which was normal to see for girls in the country but quite unusual for a woman of her obvious breeding. Though she wore the same simple riding attire most of the women on the trail chose, her dark, curling hair was arranged in a glamorous updo, as though she were headed for a fox hunt with members of state. Her face was drawn, and though Shiloh searched for it, he saw no sign of the pride and cruelty normally found in the eyes of the wealthy. She carried an air of resignation, of sadness.

"What could a woman like that be doing out here?" Joe murmured.

"Bringing trouble," Shiloh said firmly. "Better get your jaw off the ground and get those mules hitched up. Like I said, I'm gonna head to town real fast and see if I can get a few more lengths of rope." He clapped his hand on Joe's shoulder. "Woman like that's probably spoken for, and even if not, men like us have no call chasing after ladies. We'd best mind our own business."

Mister nickered and shifted beneath Ami.

"Steady, boy," she murmured, patting the gleaming brown neck.

He swiveled his ears as the lows of cattle and answering neighs of horses wafted from the cluster of wagons ahead.

Everywhere people toted, loaded, hauled and stacked. Older siblings clutched the hands of wide-eyed little ones and men barked orders to young men and in some cases, girls.

The pungent odors of sweat and animal dung filled the air. Ami was used to the scents of the stable, enjoyed them even, but something was different here. This was the stench of fear, of desperation, and she fought the urge to turn Mister and gallop away from this unknown terror. And always she fought not to look over her shoulder, for fear Father would be standing behind her, ready to drag her back home.

"Ami, is that you?" Martha Davis's round face appeared in the crowd. "Glory be!" the woman clasped her hands. "I don't believe it. I know you said you'd come, and like your mama, you're a woman of your word. But I'm flabbergasted you'd leave your fine house and life for the likes of me."

I'm not coming. I've made a terrible mistake. But Ami bit the words back as hope and relief shone from Martha's eyes. She dismounted from Mister. "Of course I came. Besides, my letter should have explained it all. I have my own reasons."

Martha grasped her hands. "Goodness child, your fingers feel like they've been plunged into a snowbank! Don't you own a pair of decent gloves?"

Ami studied her hands. "I forgot to put them on this morning. There was so much to remember." She lowered her voice, since roving eyes were beginning to settle on her and Mister. "You haven't told anyone about me, have you?"

"Of course not," Martha murmured. "I mean, I had to register you with the train, which was no small task at the last minute and all. But everyone thinks you're my sister. Come on over to the wagon and we'll talk everything out."

Ami searched for a place to tie Mister. Rows and rows of wagons fanned out before her, lined up in a semblance of order.

"Right this way, honey." Martha tugged on the sleeve of Ami's shabbiest riding habit from home. "I was fortunate to find an outfit this late. Fellow's wife died last month, and he didn't have the heart to go without her. It's a nice set-up, though a bit tight. Two wagons. He sold me ten oxen, too. Two pairs to pull at a time, and a pair to walk behind. And I've hired two men to help drive and manage them." She beamed. "Thank the Lord my home sold for a pretty penny or I don't know what we'd do."

"Sounds wonderful," Ami murmured. Though she'd graduated school with full marks, a sense of inadequacy pooled in her belly.

Martha jabbed a finger at two covered prairie schooners. The canvas gleamed with fresh white paint. "These are the ones. Aren't they lovely? I'm so happy to be heading to my husband. I miss him with every inch of my being."

Ami regarded the wagons. They seemed impossibly small when considering they must hold an entire family's worldly goods, plus food to last between towns, tents, bedding, equipment for the livestock . . . *how can we possibly do this?*

A peep inside the first schooner revealed furniture, parcels and boxes stacked from roof to rafters. The next one was fitted with a small stove, blankets, and more boxes. Ami glanced at the wagons beside them. Nothing seemed remarkably special about Martha's compared to the others, but she managed to choke out, "These seem nice."

Then she saw them. The pair of wooden trunks she'd sent with her clothing and keepsakes, set out by the side of the wagons. She'd packed as tightly as she could, but it had been difficult to fit one's entire life into such small boxes. She'd sent money to Martha to help with her share of blankets and food for the journey. *Why aren't they loaded in the wagons?*

Martha followed her gaze, and her cheeks reddened. "We didn't pack them, dearie. I didn't know for sure if you'd come, and there was no room. I thought your horse could carry them, perhaps? At least for a few days until we eat off some of the food?"

Ami's mouth fell open. "Mister? Turned into a pack mule? No." She struggled to keep her voice level.

Martha wrung her hands. "Oh, I am sorry! We might squeeze one. Heston, my youngest boy, can walk for a while or be toted. T'won't hurt him. But we absolutely can't fit them both. No one else on this trip is taking that many clothes, not even the Herschel girls." She stepped back and peered around the wagon's edge. "I'll speak to Bert and Tad, our drivers. They might be able to strap the one on the back." She scampered away with the same childish energy she'd had in the town square, a wonder for a mother of seven.

Ami sighed a deep sigh. She'd known it was foolish to pack so much. *How many clothes will I truly need in the wilds of Oregon? I can't let Mister suffer for my own vanity.* She tied his reins to the wagon rail and stared at the two trunks.

She wrenched open the first lid and peered inside. Yards and yards of China silk spilled out, all maroon with black velvet trimmings. Dorothy Anne must have slipped it in. The contrast to the simplicity and grime of her surroundings was startling, like a tropical bird in a field of starlings. A pair of women hauling a full water jug between them stopped and pointed.

Ami gathered the heavenly fabric in her arms, relishing the softness against her cheek. She scanned the rest of the trunk's contents. These were items she'd hoped to keep for her arrival in Oregon. Maybe when she was settled, she'd reasoned, she could dress in the way she'd been accustomed to. Perhaps if she found Paul . . .

You silly goose, she chided herself. *What sorts of grand balls will they be holding in Oregon?*

She removed satin slippers, darling little hats, muslin dresses with flower patterns. The trunk was too heavy to carry so she left it where it sat.

The wagons were stationed an hour's ride from Memphis. They'd congregated close to a tiny settlement with a few grouped homes and a general store. Ami remembered a little church building she'd passed on the way. She trudged by the string of wagons; countless eyes boring into her back.

The clothing was piled so high in her arms she could barely see where she was going. Thankfully, the May morning was still cool. As Ami passed the last wagon, warring thoughts buzzed through her mind. The temptation was great. *I could find someone who owns a buggy or cart of some kind. I have money. I'll load up my things, go home and ask Father for forgiveness.*

If she got on her hands and knees and begged him, maybe he wouldn't force her to marry Bernard. Two years ago, there would be no doubt where his allegiance would lie.

Somehow Millany had bewitched him and stolen his heart and mind from his own daughter. Ami stumbled along with her load, struggling to hold back tears. Self-pity wouldn't get her anywhere She must draw on the gumption given to her from both her parents. And a stubbornness that was all her own.

The church appeared before her, a tiny whitewashed building. The only indication of its purpose was a shaky and rotting steeple. The door was shut tight, but her eyes lit on a small wooden box to the side. Opening the lid revealed a few dingy rags at the bottom.

Ami gritted her teeth and shoved her entire armload of beautiful clothing and shoes into the poor box. "Good thing Dorothy Anne can't see this. She'd never forgive me."

As she straightened from her task, she locked eyes with a man on horseback across the street. His garments were fashioned from buckskin, with fringes on the sleeves and legs, but he wasn't an Indian. A floppy black hat covered his head, and a knife the length of her forearm hung from his belt. Dark, shoulder-length hair spread out over his broad shoulders from beneath his hat, and a trimmed beard covered his mouth. From where she stood, she couldn't see his expression, but he shook his head. Waves of disapproval radiated from him to her all the way across the street.

Who is he to judge me? He doesn't even know who I am. She sniffed and walked past him, determined not to let the appraising stranger make her horrible day even worse.

He didn't say a word.

She glance back again. His expression had changed, just a bit. It reminded her of how her father used to look, long ago when she was a little girl and he caught her doing something mischievous. There was disapproval, yes, but maybe just a gleam of . . . admiration?"

I don't need approval from a country bumpkin. She put her nose in the air and walked back to camp.

By the time she'd returned to the wagon train, she was already thankful for her thick shoes. Dust billowed over the tops of the leather, caught in her thick woolen stockings and rushed up to the edge of her calf-length riding habit. Sunlight streamed over the makeshift wagon settlement, promising to bring heat as it intensified.

Ami could handle the dust and the warm weather. But she wondered about the smell. She'd brought a kerchief and a small bottle of scent, but she doubted it would last throughout the journey. *Hopefully by the time I run out I'll be accustomed to it.*

Oh dear, this is dreadful. She lifted her chin and squared her shoulders. *What did you expect, Amethyst Kent? A tea party?*

She returned to the Davis's wagons, following a babble of young voices until she found the whole family lined up beside a wagon. Martha paced down the row, her jaw set as firm as the toughest sergeant.

Ellie stood at the head of the line. At seventeen, she was the oldest Davis child. She smiled shyly at Ami from beneath her yellow sunbonnet. Thin fingers clutched a tiny book to her side.

The other four children were all under the age of ten, from a rather composed girl with thick blond ringlets, the five and four-year-old boys with matching freckles like their mama's, and the baby, who had plopped himself down in the dirt and was contentedly pouring sand over his head.

Mrs. Davis nodded to Ami. "Glad you're here, dearie. The wagon master said we'll be hauling out in few moments, so we're just going over things now." She pointed to the children. "You remember Ellie, Ivy, Dan, Dave, and Heston. Children. You've met Miss Kent." She covered one side of her mouth with her hand and spoke in a stage whisper. "But we will call her Aunt Ami now."

The children stared back at her with five matching sets of blue eyes. Ami had been acquainted with them since they were babies but didn't know them very well except for Ellie, who'd been a few grades below her in school. They seemed nice enough when she'd seen them before but now a gnawing doubt chewed at the back of her mind like an insistent rat. *What do you know about children and babies? Absolutely nothing, Amethyst. Nothing.*

"No time to learn like the present," she said, and realized she'd spoken out loud. Her face grew hot and she gave a short laugh. "I suppose the heat's already gone to my head."

"You'll be just fine." Martha patted her arm. "Ellie will show you where we all plan to be when the wagons start moving. Dan and Dave are to watch the road for sticks, rocks and snakes, as well as making sure the wagon wheels stay in the ruts. You, me and Ellie will take turns driving the oxen for second wagon when the hired hands take breaks. T'other times we'll be ridin' horseback or helping Ivy with the little 'uns." She picked up Heston, who giggled and swung the small stick he'd been playing with back and forth. "Heston's going to keep out of trouble and stay alive. That's his job. Isn't it, Heston?"

"Yeth." Heston gave Ami a gapped-tooth grin and seemed oblivious to what he was agreeing to.

"Here's the money I promised you." Ami handed Martha five gold coins. "To add to the amount I've already sent you for supplies."

Martha's eyes darted to and fro as she slipped the money into her shirtwaist. "Don't be telling anyone you're paying me for this trip," she said in a low voice. "Like I mentioned before, everyone here thinks you're my sister, Miss Amethyst Tanner. That's my maiden name. Hopefully no one'll stare at us too hard, since we don't look one thing alike. My two girls know not to say anything."

"Good thinking," said Ami, as she reached into her reticule for the sweets she'd put there for the children. Her exploring fingers lit on a crumpled envelope.

"Oh dear." She slapped her forehead. "I forgot to send this letter. It's very important."

A stocky man with a graying beard strode by, followed by a gang of three other men. All were dressed in similar outfits, brown trousers with faded black vests and leather chaps.

"Yoo-hoo, Captain Reckon." Martha beckoned the stocky man over.

"Howdy, Mrs. Davis." The man tipped his dusty, wide-brimmed hat. "You and the little 'uns all set? We're pulling out at seven thirty." He drew a watch from his vest pocket and flipped it open. "Ten minutes on the dot."

"Perfectly," Martha said, smoothing her somehow immaculate apron. "Captain Reckon, I would like you to meet Miss Amethyst Tanner, my sister."

The wagon-leader held out a gloved hand. "Why lookie here, boys, we have a borned and bred lady on the trip. Pleased to make your acquaintance, ma'am."

Ami held out her hand. "The pleasure is mine, I'm sure." The polite words slipped out, but the wagon captain's leer gave her an unsettled feeling and she wished she'd said something a bit less endearing.

The wagon-master gave her hand a kiss so lingering it was almost an embarrassment. "I'll have you know, ma'am, in the twenty years I've been runnin' the trail, I've only lost a dozen souls." He leaned closer, the scent of tobacco and rotted teeth so strong her eyes smarted. "Don't you be unlucky thirteen."

"I–I'll do my best, sir," she gasped.

Captain Reckon fumbled around in a jacket pocket and pulled out two peppermint sticks. He handed one to Ami, and the other to Ellie, who shrank away. "Sweets for the sweet," he said, with a ghastly smile.

The hairs on the back of Ami's neck stood on end, but she murmured a thank you.

Martha stepped closer, pursing her lips.

Captain Reckon ignored the warning in the woman's eyes and sauntered off, whistling a tune.

"He'd better watch himself," Martha murmured. "Thought the captain of a wagon train would be respectable."

As the posse passed her, Ami tugged the sleeve of the youngest-looking member, a boy with a light fringe of beard. "Do me a favor, will you?" She pressed a dime into his hand. "Will you run this letter to the general store? I'd be most obliged, and you can keep the change."

The boy's eyes popped open. "Ma'am, that'd be five cents payment."

"No, it would be seven. Thank you so much."

"Yes, ma'am." The youth snatched the envelope and coin from her hand and ran down the street.

Hopefully the letter, filled with regret for a sudden illness that had sprung upon her, would reach Sasha Regent in the next two days, when she was expected for the grand ball. And hopefully no one else had caught wind of her being part of the wagon train. A covered wagon was about the slowest mode of transportation one could hope to find to run away with, unless one decided to travel on the back of a turtle.

5
People of the Trail

"There's a hole in my bucket,
Dear Liza, dear Liza,
A hole in my bucket.
Dear Liza, a hole."

Ami wouldn't have minded the song. And it didn't bother her that Tad, one of the oxen drivers Martha had hired, was off-key as a flock of starlings. But he'd sung the same tune endlessly, one line over and over since they started that morning. She longed for just a moment's respite. Yankee Doodle Dandy, maybe. Even Dixie would be fine, though it might cause an uproar. At least it would be different.

"There's a hole in my bucket."

If I'm forced to endure this all the way to Oregon, I'll go mad. Truly I will.

Ami trudged beside the lead oxen's head, coaxing, prodding with a stick, sometimes pushing on the yoke fastened around the beasts' necks. She'd taken over for Bert an hour ago, but it seemed like years had passed. Years filled with dust and sweat and that same infernal song.

Fortunately, the oxen needed little guidance. The massive wooden wheels stayed in the same ruts for the duration of the journey, and Bert had told her the oxen team had worked together for their lifetime.

Shouts and yells from some of the schooners fore and aft indicated that other members of the party might be dealing with more frustration than the Davis drivers.

Birds swirled in bright patterns above her head, exulting in their freedom with bursts of song.

"Hateful things to boast so!" Ami wiped her face with a handkerchief. *Thank goodness Millany can't see me right now.*

Tad's tune petered out and the wagon in front of her shuddered to a halt.

Finally, lunch time. Ami pulled back on the side of the yoke. "Woah there. Stop, stop, stop!"

The oxen continued to plod forward, their muzzles only a few yards from the back of the wagon ahead.

"Stop!" she screamed, digging her heels into the dirt.

A gloved hand wrapped around the other side of the yoke. A commanding voice boomed, "Woah, there, you big beast."

The ox came to a halt and gave a bellow, rolling big brown eyes back at her. The other oxen followed suit.

The man that she'd encountered in town from the church steps patted the ox's wide tan flank and glared at her. "If you don't know how to work with beasts, you don't have any business running a team. You're liable to get yourself killed."

The sudden fear that had jumped up Ami's throat bristled into anger. "I'll have you know; I've driven buggies and carts my entire life. My father owns some of the finest horses in Memphis."

"Be that as it may," the man gestured to the ox, "that is not a horse. Oxen are entirely different. Better tell your mother to find another driver."

Ami's skin was already clammy and hot. *By now I must look like a boiled sweet.* The updo she'd arranged so carefully before she'd stolen out of the house that morning was plastered to her head beneath her ridiculous sunbonnet. But she stuck out her chin. "My mother is dead, Mister–I didn't catch your name."

The man's scowl softened a titch. "Shiloh Talon. I'm sorry about your mother." He touched the brim of his battered black hat. "Learn how to stop an ox, will you?" He disappeared behind the row of wagons.

"Learn how to stop an ox," Ami muttered. "You should learn how to speak to a lady." She stumbled towards the back of the wagon and yelled for Bert. For all her talk, she had no idea how to unyoke the animals, and doubted she had the strength anyway.

Martha walked up with Heston sleeping on her shoulder, his curls matted with dust from the road. "Well, I'd say we've had a good start," she said in a cheerful tone. "Cold ham and potatoes for lunch. Captain Reckon says we'll wait until supper for a fire."

"Sounds fine to me." Ami's stomach erupted with hunger.

"Thank you for taking the first shift driving." Martha beckoned with her free arm for Ami to follow her around the wagon. Inside, a quilt had been spread across two small boxes, and she laid the sleeping child down with tenderness. "The children have had rougher start today than I thought they would. I'm sure they'll get used to it, but it's been nice to focus on them. Bert will be back after lunch. If you like, you can ride your horse when we get started again. We'll try to make room for Ivy to mind Heston in the wagon."

"Oh, that will be wonderful." Though she'd most likely be forced to take on some other repugnant chore instead, Ami hoped to avoid driving the oxen as much as possible, no matter how much of a brave face she had tried to put on for—what was his name? Shiloh Talon. *What kind of name is that anyway?*

Ellie pulled a large basket from the wagon. She passed out cornbread and potatoes to her siblings, who sat in a row on fallen logs beside the trail. The children devoured the food greedily.

Ami wolfed down her portion in a most unladylike manner, and then told Martha, "I'm going to stretch my legs and see if I can meet a few people."

"Good with me," Martha nodded. "My children certainly don't need help eating lunch. They can manage that just fine on their own."

Two women and a younger girl dressed in new riding habits like Ami's and wearing hats with ridiculously small brims sat in the shade of a wagon bow. Ami was surprised to see they were drinking from fragile teacups and eating from china plates, instead of the tin ones most of the people used. She considered stopping to say hello but then realized wealthy people like these might recognize her and she would rather keep that from happening until they got further down the trail. Though it would soon be inevitable.

She wouldn't have walked back this way at all if she'd realized such fine people were a part of this wagon train. *But at least they'll make it a more respectable company, won't they?* An arrow of shame pierced her heart. *Mama would never allow me to think such things. Riches certainly don't make people respectable. Look at Millany. And Bernard Regent.*

A young woman sitting on her wagon backboard bounced a baby on each knee. Dark hair flowed from beneath her kerchief like smoke, and her eyes sparkled when she smiled at Ami.

"Are they twins?" Ami asked.

"Land sakes, yes. Started walking a few weeks ago." The woman couldn't have been much older than Ami, but her body sagged with weariness. "My husband's gone to milk the cow again, we go through it like nothing. I'm Imogene, by the way. Imogene Dawson."

Ami introduced herself. "Can I help with anything?" She eyed the gabbling babies doubtfully.

Imogene shook her head. "They get fractious without me. We'll be fine." She said it as though trying to convince herself. "Thank you, though."

By the time Ami reached the end of the train, folks were packing up and getting ready to move again. *I need to return to Mister.* She couldn't wait to ride something that could move faster than a snail's crawl.

The last wagon stood slightly apart from the others. Instead of sporting a canvas cover, it was fashioned entirely from wood. Four mules were harnessed to the front. Lovely flowers, hearts and curlicues were painted around the sides. Ami leaned in to examine the writing. "A merry heart doeth good, like a medicine," she read out loud. *Sounds like a Proverb. I'm almost sure the minister gave a sermon on that verse in church once.*

"Hello!" The voice was sudden, sharp, and inhuman.

Ami nearly jumped out of her skin. She turned with caution, almost expecting to see a wizened elf or gnome. But no one stood behind her.

A flash of black moved in the shadowed corner of the wagon's overhang.

"Oh, it's a crow," she said, and laughed shakily. "I almost thought you said "hello."

The bird opened its shiny obsidian beak. "Hello!"

"Oh!" Ami pressed her hands against her cheeks. "You did say hello. Goodness!"

A woman came around the corner of the wagon, two woven baskets swinging from her hands. A smile broke out over her wrinkled face. "Yes, Archibald can say a few things in the human tongue, though his own bird language is far more expressive." The woman placed her baskets on the ledge of the wagon, and the bird hopped down and settled in the wiry gray curls that covered her bare head.

"How interesting. I've heard of parrots talking, but never a crow," said Ami.

"I raised him from a tiny thing after he fell from his nest," said the old woman. "Many people say crows are good for nothing, but he's been an admirable companion. What's more, he makes an excellent guard bird. Nothing comes around the wagon without his cordial greeting, day or night."

Archibald cocked his head and peered at Ami with a beady eye.

Ami held out her hand to the woman. "I forgot to introduce myself. I'm Amethyst . . . Tanner." The name tasted bitter and strange to her tongue, like the lie behind it.

A few thin lines appeared on the woman's forehead. "I see." She shook Amethyst's offered hand with a grip as firm as a man's.

"I'm Jerusha. Jerusha Fielder. I'm a wanderer, off to see Oregon for myself or perish in the trying." She lowered her voice. "If you have any ailments, you come to see me. I keep a passel of herbs in my wagon, medicines good for headaches and wounds of the flesh and heart, indigestion, pain and ague, consumption, and many other grievances. You aren't with child, are you?" She gave Ami's abdomen a slanted glance.

"I should say not!" Fire leaped to Ami's cheeks. "I'm not even married. I'm here with my . . . my sister."

Jerusha patted her arm. "Not trying to upset your soul, dear. I'm a midwife, by trade, so I mean to inform any woman who might need my services."

"Well, that's . . . nice," Ami managed to splutter. "I'll keep that in mind."

Jerusha laughed. "I can tell you're a lady, from a lady's home. You've probably been taught ladies don't talk about such things, that they aren't nice. Many women have suffered in silence because of this, and that's why I offer my services. Remember, if you need me for any ailment, I can help."

The sound of a bugle rose up from the head of the wagons, a call that already made Ami jump to attention.

"I need to go find Mister, my horse," she said to Jerusha. "Nice to meet you."

She picked up the short skirts of her riding habit and ran through the maze of wagons. Most of the other people were already perched on horses or wagon seats, or in their walking positions, safely out of the way of rolling wheels and ruts.

Mister nickered to her from his place at the back of the second Davis wagon. She quickly saddled him up.

###

Gratitude filled Ami's heart as she clicked her tongue at Mister and urged him past the long line of wagons. Ox-drivers and women trudging beside their little ones gave her envious glances as she rode by. Though the afternoon was a bit warm, a delicious breeze that hadn't been able to push through the dust around the ox hooves ruffled Ami's hair. *This is more like it. I could ride all the way to Oregon like this with no trouble.*

She found a small trail to the side of the wagon tracks and decided to explore. With the schooners making slow progress she felt no danger of being left behind.

A murmur of voices filtered through the trees, and she came upon a group of young people, also riding.

A girl turned in her saddle and raised a slender, gloved hand. "Hello, there, fellow traveler. Didn't I see you pass by at lunch time?"

The girl with the teacup. Ami nodded. "Please excuse me for not introducing myself then. I'm quite out of sorts."

The girl squeezed Ami's offered hand. "Aren't we all? My name is Francie Herschel. This is Thaddeus, my brother." She gestured to a young man with a neatly trimmed goatee beside her, who nodded and smiled. "And my sister, Maggie, is over there on the pony." She waved towards the girl Ami had seen with her before, who appeared to be about fifteen.

"Nice to meet you all," said Ami. "I'm Ami Tanner."

They picked their way down the forest trail, which seemed to parallel the wagon track for the most part. Francie and Thaddeus rode gleaming black geldings Ami suspected had once been a matched buggy pair.

Maggie lagged behind the group, exclaiming over every curious thing she found along the way.

"She's always like that," Francie sighed. "Ridiculous for a girl of almost sixteen." She swiveled in her saddle. "Maggie, you must stay with us. You'll get scalped by an Indian if you lag behind."

"Or eaten by a bear," Thaddeus muttered.

Maggie kicked the pony's sides, beaming as she caught up with them.

"There's so much to see out here! It's so much more interesting than our boring old town. And we haven't gone further than a few miles today. Not even close to Indian country, I reckon."

Francie gasped. "Really, Maggie, your language gets worse and worse by the moment. How would you feel if Mother heard you speak that way?"

Maggie shrugged. "Don't care. Mother's too busy with her fainting spells and headaches to mind me anyway." She shook her reins and the pony trotted off in the direction of the wagon train.

Thaddeus sighed. "The child will be the death of all of us, mark my words. A more spoiled girl you'll never meet. I pray for her safety every day."

Francie shrugged. "Mother has been far too ill to deal with her. The doctor told us it's all in her head. We begged Father to wait another year, but he's set on Oregon. He wants to start a bank there, you know. He believes it will solve all our family's problems. If we can get there, he thinks Mother will be happy again." She placed a gloved hand to her lips. "But here I am, just chattering away. What brings you to the trail?"

"Martha Davis is my sister, and she invited me to come along," said Ami.

"Martha Davis?" Francie appraised Ami's riding outfit. "She doesn't seem wealthy at all. And you–are you a young widow who married rich? But if so, why aren't you wearing black?" She tilted her head.

What is it with these people and their prying questions? "I've never been married," Ami said firmly.

Francie tapped her pointed chin and frowned.

Twigs snapped behind them, and Shiloh Talon rode up on a piebald horse with a wild mane that appeared as though it had never seen a currycomb. A shaggy black dog with pointed ears, perked to attention, bounded by his side.

As annoying as Ami's encounters with the man had been so far, she was thankful for the interruption to Francie's friendly interrogation.

"Ladies." Shiloh tilted back his hat and smiled.

"Hello, Mr. Talon," Francie said in a dulcet voice that wasn't at all in the same tone she'd just been using.

"Master Herschel." Shiloh turned to Thaddeus. "Would you be interested in a bit of hunting? The camp might like some fresh meat for supper."

"We have a wagon of provisions," Francie protested.

Shiloh dipped his head. "No disrespect, ma'am, but salt pork and potatoes get mighty tiresome after a few days." His gaze shifted to Ami. "You genteel folks may find pastries and lobster tail hard to come by out here."

"Venison will suit me nicely. I've joined hunting parties many times." Ami couldn't resist sticking her nose in the air.

Shiloh chuckled. "You have a mighty fine steed there, ma'am. I'm sure he can find his way through a hunt fairly well." His eyes narrowed, and Ami thought she detected a hint of compassion in the infinite gray depths. "But that's not a trail beast. You'll be lucky if he makes it a week."

Sudden anger, white and hot, burned behind Ami's eyes. "Mister's never faltered at a single obstacle. Why, a gentleman offered me one hundred dollars for him after he saw him jump a creek bed no other mount would take."

"I won't argue, ma'am." Shiloh thumped Thaddeus on the shoulder. "You ready for that hunt? We'll keep to this side of the trail so we won't lose our path."

Thaddeus shrugged. "I'll come along for a bit."

The two men rode off together, the shaggy dog running behind them.

"Ooooh!" Ami clutched Mister's reigns tighter. "Who does that Shiloh Talon think he is?"

Francie studied the thick fringe of bushes before her. "He's uppity for being common. But he sure is handsome."

6

A Dip into Disaster

Ami awoke with a start. Dim light shone through the thick canvas over her head. She sat up groggily, frigid air assaulting every bit of uncovered skin as the covers slid down around her.

The previous day's activities filtered into her mind, one by one. Beside her, Ellie stirred but did not wake. On the other side of Ellie, Ivy snored softly.

Ami rolled her eyes. The youngest Davis girl had kept them up chattering long into the night, until Ellie threatened to dump a bucket of water over her head. Still, she was a cheerful little thing, and Ami couldn't help but appreciate her warm presence.

Everything ached. Though Ami was no stranger to the saddle, the constant riding paired with sleeping on the hard ground with only a thin mattress between it and her body would take some getting used to. When she threw the covers off, she almost expected to look down and see bruises covering her skin from head to toe.

Fortunately, this notion was unfounded. She washed her face and hands in a pail they'd brought in the night before and dressed with stiff motions.

Everything felt slightly damp, and the ground squished beneath her feet. *We must have had a sudden shower during the night.*

Martha already had the fire stoked and breakfast ready when Ami emerged from the tent. "Here's your mush." She handed Ami a bowl of grayish, lumpy gruel. "You can have an apple as well, if you like."

Ami took the bowl and sat down on a log. She studied the thick, glue-like substance, trying not to wrinkle her nose. "Thank you for making breakfast. You could have woken me. I would have helped you."

Martha tipped her head to the side. "Don't worry about it. I always was an early riser. Sometimes it's good for me to have a bit of time in the morning all to myself without the children. Gives me space to think."

Ami choked down the full bowl of gruel, her growling stomach thanking her, though her taste buds did not. As she ate, she couldn't help but long for a plate of Nancy's flapjacks with a creamy poached egg on the side. *You've left that life behind*, she reminded herself.

Ami added her tin plate to a pile of dirty dishes in a small washtub. "I'm finished eating. Is there anything I can do now?"

"Churn butter, if you like." Martha gestured to a wooden device on the ground beside the fire.

Ami regarded the wooden item with interest. She'd seen butter churns, sure, but Nancy always ordered store-bought butter and she'd never so much as touched such an apparatus. She grasped the round staff that rose from the lid and gave it an experimental shake. Liquid sloshed inside.

Martha glanced at her. "I already filled it with milk. We're fortunate Henrietta calved this year. Had to sell the little bull early, but we'll have milk for two months or more."

Ami nodded like she understood every word, though really she didn't. Her knowledge of beasts began and ended with horses.

She tried twisting the staff, then rocked it from side to side, but not much seemed to be happening.

A peal of laughter sounded behind her. "Aunt Ami, whatever are you doing?" Ivy stood behind her, cheeks glowing with mirth.

"Churning?" Ami said meekly.

"If you do it that way, you'll end up with a churn full of sour milk." Ivy gently took the staff from her hands. "May I show you how to do it properly?"

"I suppose you ought to," Ami stepped back and watched the child industriously pump the staff up and down. "You'll probably have to teach me all sorts of things."

"I don't mind," said Ivy, with a wave of her hand.

I bet you don't. Ami smiled. What seemed like the simplest tasks evaded her. She shrugged. *I suppose I have two thousand miles to figure them out.*

After Ami helped feed the children and clean up breakfast, the bugle call sounded through camp. Time to start moving once more.

Bert and Tad had decided the womenfolk wouldn't be driving the oxen again unless it was absolutely necessary, after reports spread through camp of other women and children getting their feet stomped and one unfortunate runaway incident that led to a broken wagon tongue and one injured ox. As much as Ami detested being viewed as a member of the weaker sex, she acknowledged that she needed more practice with the oxen before she should drive them alone again. And since she really had no desire to do so any time soon, she didn't argue with Bert and Tad, whatever their reasoning.

For the morning part of the journey, she helped to rally the littles. Heston trudged on manfully in his boots, sometimes stooping to pick up pebbles and feathers. He would hold his treasures in his chubby hands for a while, and then replace them with new items he'd find.

After a time, the child would inevitably falter, and then Ami, Martha or Ellie would scoop him up and carry him for spell, until he wiggled so much they'd have to put him down again. The whole process was exhausting.

Only a few hours in, the party approached a steep embankment too wide to skirt around. The wagons stopped and Captain Reckon and his men dashed among the schooners, giving orders.

"With the rain last night, the hill is muddy and slippery," Martha explained to Ami. "They'll have to take the wagons down slowly, one at a time. We'll unload the heaviest items and carry them by hand."

Hours later, the Davis family, along with Ami, Bert and Tad, had moved everything they could from the two family wagons and stacked them at the bottom of the hill.

Ami had slipped more than once, torn her riding habit, and was covered with mud. "I've never been so filthy in all my life," she told Ellie.

"I have," Ellie replied. "But not since I was little."

Ami joined Francie and Maggie on the side of the hill to watch the first wagon ascend.

A dozen men surrounded the schooner on all sides, two positioned by the oxen and one at each of the four wheels, holding to the very rudimentary brakes. The other men were roped to the wagon's sides.

"Are they really going to keep it from sliding down by brute force?" Francie whispered.

"The teamsters have taken this hill before. I trust and hope they know what they're doing," Ami whispered back.

With a shout, the lead men began to coax the oxen down the hill. The wagon trundled after the beasts readily, as gravity took its toll.

Men holding straps dug their heels in the ground to keep the wagon from jolting into the oxen's legs. Their red faces were slick with sweat, and veins bulged from their necks. The wagon's wheels made deep ruts in the mud.

Maggie covered her eyes. "Oh, I can't watch, I afraid to death someone will be run over!"

Ami closed her eyes as well, to pray, but the prayer was short. It was hard to look away, with disaster threatening to strike at any time.

Fortunately for everyone involved, the embankment was short. Against all probability, the first wagon lighted safely at the foot. The men moved it to the side for the family who owned it to reload.

Ami glanced back where dozens more wagons waited their turn. It would be a long day.

###

After the wagons had been safely landed, with remarkably few incidents, Captain Reckon spread the word that they'd be camping at the bottom of the hill to give everyone a chance to rest and recover.

"I'm going for a ride, would you like to come with me?" Ami asked Ellie. "We can double up on Mister, he won't mind."

Ellie glanced up from the pot of dried beans she was picking through. The long walks already seemed to be taking their toll on the young girl, who was often obliged to ride in the wagon. "I'd better stay and help Mother," she said. "But ask me again sometime."

"All right." A small dart of fear pierced Ami's heart. *Will Ellie be able to survive this journey?* Countless lives had been lost along the trail. She made a vow to herself that she would step in and help Ellie with the more difficult physical tasks any chance she could.

Ami saddled up Mister and rode him down a side trail. She quickly found the Herschel siblings, just like the night before.

Before them stretched an expanse of water, surrounded by sandy bluffs, with willows and other trees growing around it.

Thaddeus took a long look at the shining lake before them and whistled. "Ladies, this would be the perfect place for a swing."

"Silly, we don't have anything of the sort," said Francie.

"Don't we though? I've brought plenty of rope and the board we used back home." Thaddeus smiled; a gesture that made a shining scar over his left cheek stand out all the more. Francie had told Ami in private that the scar was from a fall from an apple tree in the orchard. "Before the war, when they were all burned to the ground," she'd said sorrowfully.

"We used to build swings all the time at home, over our pond." Maggie shielded her eyes with her hand and gazed out over the lake. "But that was only for us, of course. When we were children."

"Maggie, you are still a child," said Francie.

"Am not." Maggie stuck out her tongue.

Ami had to admit the sturdy oak that spread its branches over the lake did appear easy to climb. And though evening was approaching, the heat still prevailed. Her dress was soaked with sweat and stuck to her shoulders.

"Hold up, I'll be back. I'll tell some of the other fellows." With that, Thaddeus was gone.

"You don't think us ladies should actually swim in the lake, do you?" Francie gestured to the water. "It wouldn't be proper. Not one bit."

Ami fanned her face with a broad leaf from the oak. "Why not? We'll wear our petticoats. And we won't go on the swing with the boys. We can stay down in the water. Over there." She pointed to a quiet inlet, almost completely surrounded by trees. "The fellows are gentlemen. They won't bother us. Hurry, let's go before they get back."

"Oh yes, please." Hope filled Maggie's round, angelic face. "I'm dying of heat, Francie, really, I am."

"Oh, we might as well." Francie began to pull off her riding gloves. "Thaddeus won't let anything happen to us. He's vexing at times, but he always keeps us safe."

The three girls tied their horses to a sturdy log, and they slipped down the muddy bank, giggling. Joy rose in Ami's spirit. The past days had been filled with back-breaking chores, more difficult work than she'd ever done in her life, though she felt like Martha had kept her from the worst of it for fear she'd give up and go back home.

An evening swim seemed divine, when the closest thing she'd had to a bath on this trip was a shallow bucket of tepid water and a bar of homemade lye soap.

The inlet was cool and lovely as it had promised to be, with long strands of Spanish moss dipping into the water from willow trees growing along the bank. Late spring flowers peeped through thick stands of grass that almost completely concealed them from the shore. Here and there a cricket chirped, rehearsing for nightfall.

Thaddeus returned with the swing and several of the younger men. Soon the girls heard shouts and splashes as they dared each other to do death-defying feats of acrobatics that would surely have broken their necks if attempted.

Maggie stood in the water, listening. "Sounds like they're having fun," she said in a wistful voice.

Ami floated on her back, her dark hair swirling around her like a gossamer shawl. "The boys can keep their old swing," she said. "I prefer our little cove here."

"Me too." Francie, swam with placid strokes, her hair still somehow in a perfect updo, without a drop of water to mar it.

Someone crashed through the bushes, and a tanned face peeped out through the trees. "Girls, what on earth are you doing?"

Maggie screamed long and loud, and clutched at her chest, though her petticoats were many and nothing below her neck was visible through the lake water.

"Shiloh Talon, leave our cove this instant." Ami stood on her tiptoes and tried to look as firm as possible, though her feet sank in the mud and threatened to slip out from beneath her.

"Oh, I will," Shiloh's eyebrows were drawn down over his nose, but the corner of his mouth twitched. "As soon as I tell you about the snake I just saw glide into the lake."

The water erupted. Francie and Maggie flailed and screamed, pushing past each other to be the first to get to shore. Ami followed a bit more sedately. Ol' Pat had taught her everything he knew about woodcraft over the years. The water snakes in this area were probably not venomous. *Still wouldn't be desirable to have one up my petticoat.*

True to his word, Shiloh was gone by the time the women reached the shore.

Francie and Maggie grabbed their dresses, wrapped them around themselves as best they could, and scurried off in the direction of the wagon train.

Ami pulled on her habit, stiff with sweat and dirt, and looked back longingly at the water. Suddenly one small snake didn't seem like much of a threat.

On the way back to camp, Shiloh stepped out of the woods, his dog, as always, beside him.

"Wasn't my intention to give you girls a fright," he said gruffly. "Didn't know any other way to tell you. I was surprised a lady like you would take a dunk at all."

"My father might have money, but that doesn't mean I don't enjoy a nice swim." A sudden breeze hit Ami's still-wet petticoats and she shivered.

A rare grin spread across Shiloh's face. "I wonder what your father would think of you now."

Ami crossed her arms. "My father was far too busy for me, Mr. Talon. Unless he was trying to show me off to his rich friends or pawn me off to the highest bidder." She moved up the trail with quick, irritated steps.

"That doesn't sound like an enviable life," Shiloh strode faster to stay by her side. "But surely you could have found another way besides running off to Oregon."

Ami stopped short, and her heart caught in her throat. "Please," she half-whispered. "Please don't tell anyone."

"Hey, you pretty much told me yourself." Shiloh stepped in front of her, his dark eyes snapping. "It's your business, not mine, but you need to be careful." He glanced around them. "Ruthless men walk this trail, and if they find out you're a wealthy runaway they might take the opportunity. Some don't care which way riches lie. They will chase the biggest coin purse."

Ami frowned. "First you predict the demise of my horse, and now you're giving me dire warnings about the trail." She sighed. "But I will be careful, Mr. Talon."

"Please, I'm Shiloh. Even the Indians call me that." Shiloh smiled again and touched her hand. "Let's be friends, shall we? I won't tell your secret. I promise. And I'll watch out for you."

Ami wanted to say she could watch out for herself, thank you very much, but the crippling shock of how easily her secret had floated out still held her in a death grip. "Thank you," was all she could choke out.

Shiloh's eyes held depths of words unsaid, but he whistled to his dog and disappeared into the woods.

7
Danger in the Night

Smoke, thick and acrid, filled Ami's nose and she sat up, almost hitting her head on the wagon ribs above her. They'd made camp by a stream but due to earlier rain there'd been plenty of mosquitoes, so the women and children had pushed out some of the furniture and chests to sleep inside the wagon. It was hot, dank, and so crowded Ami felt she was surrounded by a litter of puppies, but she preferred this arrangement to being eaten alive.

Shouts of men filled the air, along with the screams of horses and oxen.

"Mister!" Ami crawled past drowsy children and a wide-eyed Martha.

The woman grabbed her arm as she passed.

"Ami, be careful! Might be Indians!"

"The wagon master said the Indians in this area are friendly," Ami protested. "Let me go, I need to see what's happening."

She yanked away from Martha's terrified grasp and pushed her head through the wagon flap.

The night air was filled with a rancid red smoke that poured itself down Ami's throat. Covering her mouth and nose with her arm, she remembered that while she was wearing more by way of night clothing than she would have at home, she still wasn't what folks would call decent. *Not much to be done about that if our lives are in danger. Decency will have to take a second fiddle.*

She stumbled out of the wagon, blinking in the dark, smoky night. The wagons were a few lengths apart, rising like giant loaves of bread around her.

Mister gave a shrill whinny from where he'd been tethered in the thick grass a few yards away. Ami ran to him. He reared back, the whites of his eyes gleaming in the star light.

"I know, I know, sweetheart." She grabbed his halter and stroked his nose. "I'm going to find out what's wrong. Maybe a child put green wood on a fire again."

A red glow filled the sky. *That's not a campfire.*

Ami's knees started shaking. "Martha!" she shrieked. "Hitch up the oxen! You might need to move the wagons!"

Martha stuck her head outside the flap. "I don't know how! And I can't find Tad or Bert!"

"Get the children dressed then. We may need to get away in a hurry. I think one of the wagons is on fire. I'll try to find the drivers." Ami picked up the skirts of her nightdress and ran down the row of wagons.

The smoke thickened and the air became harder to breathe. Men rushed past her. Though every instinct she possessed warned her not to take another step, she pushed closer to the fire.

"The Dawson wagon," she whispered.

Flames leapt from the wagon cover, sparks zipping into the night like crazed fireflies.

Men and women beat at the flames with blankets, and lines of children were passing buckets, tin cans, anything that could hold water from the nearby stream.

A man elbowed her as he came by, dragging a thick woolen blanket. "I heard the kids are still inside." He shook his head. "Mr. Dawson was sleeping outside in a tent. He got burned real bad trying to go in after em'. No sign of Missus Dawson either."

Ami gasped. The wagon would be a death trap if the cover became engulfed.

"Someone has to go in there!" She tried to get closer to the schooner, but the heat was too intense. "We can't let them die!" she screamed.

"We won't." Shiloh came up beside her, his lips set in a grim line. He grabbed a blanket from a man who'd been beating the flames, then ran to the water line. "Give me a bucket!"

A trembling child handed him a pail.

Shiloh pushed the blanket down into the bucket, and pulled it out again, dripping wet.

The thin cry of a baby drifted from the prairie schooner.

"Hurry, Shiloh! Oh, hurry!" Ami cried.

Shiloh threw the blanket over himself, sped past her and disappeared into the wagon.

A man wailed from the crowd. "Imogene, Oh, Imogene! Please, come back to me!" Ami assumed this was Mr. Dawson, but she couldn't tell through the smoke.

In the next eternally long moments, the crowd continued to beat at the fire and douse the flames with water, though each bucket seemed like a fly spitting on a horse.

Ami kept her eyes fixed on the wagon flap. *Will Shiloh die trying to save the babies?*

Suddenly, the canvas side of the wagon was slashed open. A baby emerged through the hole, crying and covered with soot. A woman rushed forward and grabbed the child. Another baby appeared, and another member of the crowd braved the searing heat to catch him.

Finally, the blanket-covered Shiloh emerged from the wagon, dragging out a motionless woman.

Ami's throat tightened from fear and smoke, and she thought she might never breathe again.

The wailing man pushed his way forward, his hands bound in strips of muslin. "Oh, Imogene, Imogene!"

Jerusha emerged from the night, her hair wild and eyes glowing in the light of the fire. "Bring her over to the water!" Two men took Imogene from Shiloh, and the man collapsed in a heap on the ground.

Captain Reckon rushed forward and barked, "Come on folks, those who don't have to tend to the hurtin' come put this fire out. We are all still in danger!"

Ami pushed her way through the throng, trying to reach Shiloh's side. By the time she got to the place where he'd collapsed, he was gone. She made her way to the stream's edge.

Shiloh was there, sitting on a log, holding one of the twins. The baby, seemingly unhurt, gazed up at him with solemn eyes.

Ami put her hand on his shoulder. "Are you all right? That was a dangerous thing to do . . . but so brave."

"They were all curled up together, like baby birds in a nest. I couldn't let them die." Shiloh gave her a wilder look than she'd seen in the eye of any human being. "Could I?"

"Of course not," she said in what she hoped was a soothing voice. *But the rest of us nearly did.* The thought brought a sour taste to her mouth, and she focused on the baby instead.

"My mother. Died in a fire." Shiloh studied the small group of women who had joined Jerusha in trying to revive Imogene. "My father saved me instead of her."

"Oh, Shiloh. That's terrible." The enormity of the situation began to wash over Ami, and she rocked slightly in her seat.

"Here, will you take him?" Shiloh held out the child. "I'm gonna go help the others."

"Of course." Ami took the squirming bundle and craned her neck to see what was happening with Imogene. "Your mama will be just fine and dandy," she told the baby, hoping it would be true.

At long last, Imogene stirred, moving her arm.

Ami breathed a sigh of relief. The baby wrinkled his nose and she laughed, "Sorry, I had onions for dinner."

She held the infant close while the men put out the rest of the fire. The wooden frame stuck out through the flames in a somber silhouette.

A ragged cheer rose up as the last flame was doused. Here and there a man stomped an ember with a heavy boot.

The baby cooed and sucked at his fingers.

"I bet your mama wants to see you," Ami whispered.

She carried him to the little crowd huddled around Imogene.

The moon shone serenely on the glassy surface of the water, as though nothing had happened. Here and there, tiny water creatures jumped and splashed, and then all was still again.

Mr. Dawson sat beside his wife, his eyes glassy, and his jaw slack, as though he were off in another land, a place where his family had never been in danger and all his possessions had been lost in mere moments. He seemed much older than Imogene, close to his forties. His hands, still wrapped in their hasty bandages, rested in his lap and his body shook violently.

A woman Ami didn't recognize held the other twin. The little boy's hair, once thick and curly, had been mostly singed off but he seemed fine besides.

Jerusha placed wet cloths on Imogene's forehead and glanced up at Ami.

"Is she going to be all right?" Ami asked in a low voice.

Jerusha's mouth drew into a tight line. "Hard to say. Breathed in a mighty bit of smoke, the stuff can destroy a body from the inside out. But she's young and strong, and survived birthin' these two young 'uns together. I think she'll pull through." She patted the baby's head. "She won't have to mourn the loss of her babies, and I'd say that'd be more deadly than any fire."

Imogene's eyes fluttered open. "Where is my Samuel?" she murmured, her eyes roving from side to side. "Oh, my poor little Sam. Mommy's sorry she forgot to put out the fire in the stove. Oh Sam! Isaac? Where are my babies?"

"Don't you fret." Jerusha beckoned to Ami, who scooted a bit closer. "Your precious babies are right here. We'll take the whole four of you to my wagon tonight so I can tend to you and give you medicine."

"Would you like me to come and help?" asked Ami. "I don't know much about babies, but I can stir soup and change bandages. I wouldn't be able to sleep anyway."

"Of course you can come," said Jerusha. "It's been a long night, and I fear it will only stretch the longer until morning breaks."

###

The next morning was Sunday. From the first day, Captain Reckon had established they would only travel during the Sabbath in desperate times, for instance, if there was no source of water close by. But even if it had been any other day of the week they would have remained at camp, because of the Dawson's fire.

Men and women spoke in hushed conversations and children who became too loud at play were scolded into silence. Word from Jerusha's wagon was hopeful. Mr. Dawson's burns were not serious and should heal nicely, and Imogene would make a full recovery if she could rest for a few more days. The twins, amazingly, were fine.

The wagon teamsters huddled in groups or strode around the camp with grim frowns. Everyone knew what they were thinking. The wagon train was already running a few days behind schedule, though they'd slipped into Iowa the day before. They could not afford to stay in one place for long.

And what if they did wait? The Dawson family had lost their only wagon, along with most of their money and belongings. All that remained were the scant, singed clothes on their backs, three teams of oxen and a horse. They couldn't continue the journey. Most folks saved for years for an Oregon outfit. Even if Mr. Dawson found a wagon for sale in one of the towns along the route, affording one would be impossible.

The sabbath service was somber. Thaddeus pulled out a violin and played a few hymns, strong and sweet. Sniffles came from many in the group, and Ami shed a few tears of her own, thinking of her friends she'd left behind, maybe forever. Especially Dorothy Anne, Brenda and Ol' Pat.

Mr. Dawson shuffled to the group, his head bowed low. His hands were freshly bandaged.

Ami caught Thaddeus staring at Mr. Dawson's hands, and then his own, holding his fiddle and bow.

So much to be thankful for. A lump formed in Ami's throat. *Surely God's favor is upon us. Three fresh graves would have been dug this morning if it weren't for Shiloh Talon.*

Shiloh stood near the edge of the group, a few yards apart from his nearest neighbor. He wore the usual buckskins, but the battered hat was gone and his unruly hair had been wetted down and perhaps even combed. His eyes were closed, and he seemed to be . . . praying, perhaps? He appeared to be in a world of his own, so private that Ami's cheeks reddened and she turned away. She wouldn't have pegged the man to be much of a churchgoer, but he'd already surprised her more than once on the trail.

Jerusha wasn't among the congregation, because she was still caring for Imogene and the children. Ami had been relieved by another caring soul in the wee hours of the morning. As the music played on, she struggled to stay awake. Thankfully, they'd done extra tasks the day before to rest on the Sabbath as much as possible.

That evening Martha brushed a tear from her eye as she and Ami snapped peas and threw them in a cast-iron pot full of boiling water. "It's a shame, that's what it is. Imogene barely remembered her own name she was so sleep deprived. Why, any of us could have left the stove burning. I was always nervous about those little sheet stoves, I have one, but I prefer to do most of my cooking outside."

"What do you think they'll do?" asked Ami.

"I overheard the wagon master tell Bert we're leaving in the morning. The Dawson family will just have to hunker down here on this section of trail until they're better. Someone's giving them a small cart so they'll have provisions to get back to town. Thank goodness we're only five days out. The Henderson boy will be helping them along for a day or two until they reach that last little settlement we passed, and then he'll gallop back to us on that mustang of his."

"I suppose it's the only way," murmured Ami.

"It wasn't God's will for them to go to Oregon." Martha shook her head. "That reminds me. The ladies are trying to collect some things to help them out. I have an extra bag of potatoes. It's not much, but when everyone throws something in the pot you can make a stew. Would you mind taking it to Jerusha's wagon for me?"

"Not at all. Maybe I have something I could give too."

Ami went into the wagon and crawled to the far corner where they'd buried her one small trunk. When she opened it, she was overwhelmed by the scent of gingersnaps, lavender and cigars. The smell of her father's house.

She'd only been gone for five days, but the scent was like a strong arm, yanking her into the past. Away from the dust, the stench. The eternal creaking of the wagons.

I paid for my supplies. I could ride Mister home now. A single horse and rider could make it to town in a few days. There's bound to be a respectable boarding house in one of those towns I could stay at. It's like Shiloh said. Someone's likely to figure out who I am. They'll send word to my father and he'll be after me like a shot. If he isn't already.

Bernard Regent's smirk, pasted across those thick lips, broke into her reverie. As miserable as some of these moments had been on the trail, someday she'd find an end to the hardships. They'd reach Oregon and she'd create a new life for herself. *With Paul.* She caught her breath. *Or someone. Or even if I'm alone, I'd rather be a spinsterly teacher than hitched to Bernard and the rest of the Regent clan forever.*

Ellie peeked her head in. "Ma was wondering if you'd gone yet. She says we're leaving in a quarter hour."

"Be right out."

Ami reached into her trunk and pulled out a shirtwaist, far too nice for daily life on the trail. Waterfalls of lace spilled from the sleeves and throat.

She examined the garment. Not practical, but a pretty thing for a woman who had nothing. *They might even be able to sell it.*

She wrapped it in paper and dashed to the end of the wagon train. Most of the schooners were ready to leave, with oxen and the few mules standing patiently in yokes and harnesses.

The small cart that had been donated to the Dawson family was at the very end of the line, set apart like a tag-along child. Imogene rested in the shade with the twins on her knees, much like the first day Ami had met her.

As Ami approached the setup, she noticed the smoothness of Imogene's forehead, the youthful glow to her cheeks. *How terrible to have suffered through such an event at her age. But at least she didn't lose her husband or children.*

"Hello, Imogene," Ami said. "I hope you're feeling better."

"I am." Imogene glanced up, and all the years Ami had missed where there, gathered in her eyes. "Thank you for helping Jerusha the other night."

"I'm so . . ." Ami struggled for the right words. "Sorry. That you can't go on."

Imogene gave a mirthless laugh. "Don't be. To tell you the truth, this was David's dream. I never wanted to come out here, at least while the babies were so young. They say in a few years, the railway will bring everyone across the west. Maybe we'll try again someday." She patted a baby's back. "Until then, my mama will be glad to see me. I've never seen her cry so hard as when we left."

"I'm glad you have family waiting for you," said Ami. "God be with you."

Ami handed Imogene her package. "Something for you, and Martha sent this bag of potatoes."

"Thank you." Imogene nodded to the cart. "Would you mind putting them in there?"

Ami added the items to a very small pile of pots, food and sparse articles of clothing the other members of the train had given. *So little.* But the general generosity of folks was being held back by fear. The trail was so long, and they'd only just started.

She twisted her head towards Imogene. The woman was wearing an ill-fitting dress someone had donated, and she shivered in the chill of morning. The babies still wore the clothes they had slept in, singed and smoky.

A memory flashed into Ami's mind from when she'd been eight or so. She and her mother were stepping out of church on a wintry morning. Snow fell thick and hard, covering the world in billowing drifts. Ami was terribly proud of a beautiful new fur muff made of gray rabbit fur she'd received for Christmas. All her friends had envied the beautiful thing, and she'd worn it just a bit longer than necessary in the church.

As her mother led her to their waiting coach, Ami caught sight of a family on the church steps. People from every walk of life attended the community place of worship, so Ami was used to seeing rich and poor folks sharing the same pews. But this family appeared to be especially destitute. One little girl had especially dirty, unkempt hair, and her coat was full of patches and holes. She glanced at Ami and then covered her face.

Ami tugged on her mother's dress. "Mama, see that little girl? Why doesn't she have something warmer on?"

Her mother bent down and said "Perhaps God wants to give you the blessing of helping her today. Would you like that?"

"But what can I give, Mama?" Ami's eight-year-old eyes widened.

"What would you like to give, my dear?" her mother searched her face with kind eyes.

"I have my muff." Ami's little world crashed down around her ears. "But if I give this, my hands will be cold. And she'll get it all dirty, Mama. I know she will."

Her mother had smiled a gentle smile. "Of course, Ami. You don't have to give it up. I know you love it so. Let's see if we can give one of the warm blankets in our coach." She turned to open the buggy's door.

While her mother rummaged through the coach, a peace filled Ami's heart, and she removed the muff from her hands and thrust it into the little girl's arms. "This is for you," she said.

Ami blinked and studied the cart once more. Then she slowly unwound her mother's shawl from around her shoulders. She'd have to find another way to keep out the chill in the morning, and it was so, so hard to let go of anything that had belonged to Mama. *Inasmuch as ye have done to the least of these . . .*

She draped the woolen wrap around Imogene's shoulders, and tucked the corners around the babies. "It's old, but it should keep you warm. And here." Pulling out her precious coin pouch, she found a five-dollar gold piece and handed it to Imogene.

Imogene's mouth sagged. "I–I can't take this."

"Don't you tell a single soul where you got it," Ami warned her. "Except your husband, and you can tell him after we leave."

Imogene's lips trembled. "I won't. I promise."

As Ami returned to the Davis wagons, she glanced behind her at the tiny cart and the family gathered around it, like kittens huddled with a mother cat. "God, please keep them safe on their journey. And let Imogene see her mama again soon."

8
A Visit to Town

On the eighth day, the wagon train arrived on the outskirts of Chariton, Iowa. Martha pressed three pennies into Ami's hands. "would you take this letter for my husband into town and mail it? Hopefully it will reach him before I do."

Ami hesitated. "I would enjoy going back to civilization for a day, but what if my father has sent word or scouts to look for me?"

Martha wrinkled her nose. "Are you that worried? How would anyone you'd gone off to Oregon? That would be the last thing I'd think a young lady of your rank and breeding would do. No offense to you, my dear, and I'm more than thankful you're here with us, but unless someone in the outfit figures it out from within, I imagine you're safer than safe." She fanned a cloud of flour from her apron. "Not to mention we went a different route than most because of the Indian problems. Most folks go straight through to

Nebraska, they don't take the Iowa road. Captain Reckon made a last-minute decision."

"That's true." Ami took the letter. "I'll go. I wanted to see about some perfumed soap in the general store. I've missed mine something fierce and can't believe I forgot to pack even one bar."

Martha smiled a dreamy smile. "Rose petal soap would be heavenly. I'd bathe all the babies with the stuff, perhaps it would keep the stench down when we have to sleep in the wagon."

"I'll buy an extra bar if I find it," Ami promised.

Ellie fell in step with Ami as she headed to the town. "Mama said I might walk with you if you're obliged. I long for a break from the little 'uns and I'm feeling stronger today."

"Of course you can come with me. And I don't blame you. Your brothers and sister are sweet, but they can be vexing."

Ellie's face lit up beneath the light dusting of freckles scattered over her nose. "Thank you, Miss Ami."

"Don't forget, you're always welcome to come along when I go riding," Ami said as they picked their way over wagon ruts and rocks in the wide road. "I'm sure your mother would allow you to ride her bay pony or we could scare you up another horse somewhere. Maggie isn't much younger than you. I bet the two of you could have a merry time."

"Pardon me for saying," Ellie glanced down, her white-blond eyelashes brushing her cheeks, "but being similar ages doesn't always make someone your friend."

"True," Ani said ruefully, thinking of Millany. "Sorry, I thought you might enjoy something fun."

"Fun?" Ellie gave a short laugh. "Don't have much time for fun, not with three young 'uns to care for. I should be thankful though. By the time my mama was my age she was married and carrying me in her belly. I'm glad I'm a daughter only, and not a wife." She lowered her voice, and Ami had to bend closer to catch the almost whispered words. "Sometimes, though, when I'm washing dishes, or minding the littles, I go away to places in my head. I can be whatever I want. A princess, or a teacher. Sometimes I even pretend I'm a native from faraway lands with a gold ring in my ear, riding an elephant." She stepped back with a defiant look, as though she expected Ami to be scandalized.

"I played pretend too," Ami said. "Especially when I was out riding my horse, Mister. Sometimes I pretended to be a great general of an army. Or we'd jump fences and I'd imagine I was a part of a steeplechase race, like the ones they have in England."

Ellie fiddled with the end of her blond braid. "I guess I won't be riding elephants any time soon. Not with my constitution. And I doubt a man will want to marry a weak thing like me."

Ami lifted her chin. "There's nothing wrong with pretending. And don't ever let anyone tell you otherwise."

Ellie shrugged. "No one can force us to think a certain way. That's the beauty of things." She kicked a small pebble and it bounded across the road, landing in a puddle with a tiny splash. "I overheard Shiloh say something about you, but I probably shouldn't tell since it's wicked to eavesdrop."

Ami's cheeks grew hot. "Well, gossip is also rude. Shiloh shouldn't talk about me behind my back."

"We-ell, it wasn't mean or nothing, Miss–I mean Aunt–Ami. He told Mother your horse was looking a bit poorly and if Mister belonged to him, he'd give him an extra measure of oats. And then he told Mama your horse wouldn't last the trail."

"He did, did he? That know-it-all." Ami bit back the stream of angry words threatening to spill out, remembering that Shiloh had promised to be her friend. And there was the matter of him saving the lives of three people only days before.

Ellie nodded. "He said your horse is a goodly beast for every day, but not for this journey. He suggested you sell him here in town and find a better horse."

Ami's shoulders stiffened. "Mister is the best horse this side of the states. I'd rather sell my own arm from my body."

Ellie smiled wistfully. "I owned a dear kitty. He'd curl up in my bed and loved only me. We had to leave him behind." A tear ran down the side of her cheek, making a trail through the dust and freckles. "Mama said he'd run away and get killed by coyotes if we brought him with us. He stayed with my best friend, who loved him, but he didn't love *her*." She glanced up quickly. "You know, don't you?"

"Oh, I'm sorry, Ellie." Ami held back the urge to put her arm around the frail shoulders. She wasn't sure how the shy girl would respond.

The village was moderately sized, with large yards sectioned off by sawed-off logs. The streets were made of dirt, unlike the cobblestone roads of Memphis. A few false-fronted businesses displayed their wares in hopeful windows.

A small group of women chatted in a cluster by the dry-goods store where Ami and Ellie headed. They smiled at the girls.

A plump woman with a green dress held up a hand in greeting. "How many days on the trail, Girls?"

"How did you know?" Ami asked.

"Oh, we get trail blazers in town almost every day," said an elderly woman. She wore a silk hat with a large black bird perched on it. Ami thought at first she might have a pet like Jerusha, but the bird remained motionless and she realized it was stuffed.

"Of course." Ami tried to peel her eyes away from the women's clothes, which would have seemed shabby next to the clothes she'd wear at home, but now seemed downright fancy when compared to her dusty riding habit that she remembered, to her chagrin, hadn't been properly washed in three days. *The thing could probably stand up on its own hem by now.* To her horror, she realized that she probably smelled awful.

Mumbling something about the lovely weather, she grabbed Ellie's hand and headed for the general store. *The sooner we pick up some of that scented soap the better.*

Though it had been less than nine days since she'd been in a place of business, Ami felt as though she'd stepped into a cave of wonders. She gazed at the bunches of dried herbs hanging from the ceiling along with plump strings of cured beef and sausage. Bolts of cloth lined one wall, and cheaply made dresses graced the storefront window, sharing space with hats and kerchiefs and other frippery. Her trunk was still filled with these items, so she paid them no mind.

She rushed to a basket filled with items of her soul's longing. Bars of plainly wrapped scented soap were stacked to the brim. Picking one up, she inhaled deeply, not caring how addled in the head she must appear. *Lavender.* Perhaps she could rig it up on a ribbon tied around her neck and wear it always.

Someone chuckled behind her. "They always go for the soap first."

She spun around. A balding man in an apron had appeared behind the counter. He rubbed his hands together and peered into her face. "What brings a lady like you out on the trail, Miss?"

"Oh, the thrill of adventure," she said a bit absent-mindedly. "And my sister . . . needed my help. Ellie, we'd better get what we want and head back. Wagon master said no one should dawdle."

"Yes, Aunt Ami." Ellie murmured. She was staring at a beautiful comb made of tortoiseshell. "Mother wanted me to buy her a spool of white thread." She tore her eyes away from the women's toiletry items and obediently selected the item. "I think this will do."

Ami piled four bars of soap on the counter, along with the thread and peppermint sticks for the children. She shouldn't spend so much, especially right away, but if she didn't have something to ward of the smell she might just die, and where would her money get her then?

At the last moment she slipped the tortoiseshell comb on the pile. Ellie's surprised smile was worth the extra dime.

The shopkeeper's grin broadened with every item she added. "You take care of yourself, Miss." He wrapped up her purchases in plain brown paper. "The trail creates no friends, and it makes no enemies. It is what it is. Our lives and destinies are forever tied up in the will of the Almighty."

One morning, a week after they'd gone to town, rain pelted the sides of the tent. When Ami pushed the covers back, the tops of the quilts were soaked. "Ooh, I guess we'll be drying these out this afternoon," she groaned.

She found Martha inside the wagon, poking at a fire she'd kindled in the sheet stove.

"This don't bode well," Martha said in a grim tone. "Wagon master said we'd be moving come wind or rain this week, we need to make up time since we started so late in the year."

"He would really have us travel in this rain?" Ami grabbed a piping-hot Johnny cake from under a cloth and took small bites, rolling the grainy substance over her tongue. The idea was ludicrous. They'd be covered in mud from which there would be no cleaning.

"We started a week later than most folks do, and the rain could continue for days." Martha stirred a pot of porridge on the top of the stove. "Let's wake the young 'uns and get them ready. No one is to ride in the wagons today, due to the oxen having to pull through the mud." She glanced at Ami's face. "No reason for woe. The hand of the Almighty is for us. I'd rather go through a bit of mud than a blizzard because we reached Oregon too late."

Ami dressed quickly and roused the children out in the tents. They yawned, rubbed their eyes, and crawled into the wagon to huddle around the stove and eat breakfast.

A commotion met Ami's eyes as she swung down from the wagon. Mr. Granbury, the owner of the schooner behind them, struggled with his youngest ox. The beast, usually a snowy white, was splattered with mud up to his chest. The animal bellowed and rolled his eyes as Mr. Granbury and two other men tried to force the wooden yoke around his neck.

"Poor thing," Ami said. "Probably doesn't like the rain either."

Captain Reckon came to stand beside Ami. "They'd better get him set straight or we'll be eating him for dinner. Sometimes these oxen learn to balk and there's no fixing them."

He glanced at Ami, rain pouring down his hat and splashing on his shoulders. "You're sure looking pretty, Miss Tanner."

Ami stiffened and looked away without replying. Captain Reckon's advances had become more forthright every day, though the man was twice her age. She figured he picked a woman to fancy for every journey. A man in his occupation wouldn't have a chance to settle down, and desperation might overtake propriety. She had no intention of becoming a story he'd tell in some saloon.

The shouts of the men became more frenzied as they worked with the ox. Mr. Granbury jumped out of the way in time to miss a well-aimed kick. The ox lowered its head and swung its sharp horns from side to side.

Jerusha moved through the quickly gathering crowd. Ami hadn't seen her in several days, and she'd forgotten how tiny the lady was. A head shorter, at least, than any grown woman in camp. Her colorful cloak and skirts made her stand out like a prairie flower among the grasses.

The elderly woman watched the men struggle with the ox, her frown deepening. At last she stepped forward.

"Gentlemen, I have a suggestion to make."

Mr. Granbury wiped his brow and glared at Jerusha. "Everyone has ideas," he growled. "And what would you suggest?" Every word dripped with frustration and contempt.

"Pull that yoke back and try to hold the beast steady." Quick as a hummingbird, Jerusha moved forward, somehow darting between horn and hoof. She examined the ox's neck.

"As best as I can tell, this creature has a horrible yoke sore here," she said, stepping back and wiping rain from her face. "Mr.

Granbury, have you not used the leather cushions? They might take a bit more time to set in place, but the care of this animal is surely worth it, don't you think?"

Mr. Granbury's face turned scarlet. "Woman, are you telling me how to keep my team?"

Jerusha squinted up at the man, who towered over her by at least two feet. "I'd suggest you use a bit of my healing salve. There's a batch in my wagon if you want it. I'd give that ox a rest for at least three days. Otherwise, you'll be eating him in a week, if there's any flesh left on his bones. He's already looking poorly."

She turned on her heel and marched back in the direction of her wagon, disappearing through a gray curtain of rain.

Captain Reckon checked the beast's neck and his shoulders sagged. "Far be it from me to tell you what to do with your animal, Mr. Granbury, but I'd skip the salve and go right to the slaughter. The wound looks septic and it already has the stench."

"You're all headed for the madhouse." Mr. Granbury spat a large wad of tobacco. "My boys and I will teach this beast a lesson, and ain't none of you gonna tell me my business." He glared at the crowd. Everyone began to mumble and walk away.

"Suit yourself," said Captain Reckon between clenched teeth. "But we're moving out now. You can catch up when you get your wagon situated."

"We'll lose our place in the train," Mr. Granbury protested.

"And that's your business, isn't it?" Captain Reckon stomped off, mud splashing over his boots with every step.

"Aw." Mr. Granbury spit a wad of tobacco into the mud. "Let's get this varmint tied to the back and bring up old Jethro. He's rested long enough."

Ami headed to the front of Martha's lead schooner, trying to ignore the bellows of the poor ox. She'd already become accustomed to seeing animals treated badly on the trail, but it still pained her heart every time. Especially because Jerusha seemed so confident the animal's ailment could be cured. And the oxen were such gentle and patient animals, lugging their heavy loads for miles every day with little in return.

Bert and Tad had already yoked up the lead oxen and were working on the second team.

"Everything all right?" Tad asked. He was as tall and lean as a stalk of prairie grass, with a thatch of dull blond hair that was now plastered to his head from the rain.

"Granbury's having trouble again. We're moving out any minute," Ami said. The oxen's flanks shivered as cold drops of rain pelted them.

"Granbury's an old fool." Bert gave the yoke one last tug and stepped back. "He ain't gonna make it past Nebraska. A righteous man has regard for his beast, and he don't care about nothing in this world that's breathin' 'cept for hisself."

"You'd think Captain Reckon would do something about it," said Martha, who had come up beside Ami.

Bert's shoulders shifted up, then down. "Captain Reckon don't have say over another man's property, whether he's beating his ox or his wife. That's the way of the trail. Every man has to go by the trail code, since we ain't got a sheriff or any sort of law to abide by out here."

"Mooooove out!" The call ran up and down the wagon train, muffled by the rain.

Thus began the most miserable two days of Ami's life until that point. Wagons became rutted in the mud and every available hand would have to work to pull them out. Children slogged beside their respective schooners or huddled beneath tarps. The wagons made such slow progress that when they stopped for a meal, they could sometimes catch a glimpse of the place they had stopped before. This was the most disheartening thing of all.

On the second day, Bert had to assist so many other folks that Ami was forced to drive the second wagon while Martha herded children through the rain.

As Ami tugged the tired oxen's yokes she wondered how travelling through this rain could possibly be worth this effort. Could this really be worse than dealing with a bit of snow at the end? Then she remembered the horror stories of the Donnor party, twenty years back, who'd lost most of their crew after arriving in California too late. She shivered. Despite his drawbacks, Captain Reckon knew this trail like very few other trail bosses. If he believed they should push forward, then they must.

Finally the wagons stopped. Everyone scrambled to set up the driest possible shelters.

Ami squinted at the sky. At least the rain seemed to be letting up.

A man strode by, a dog at his heels. Though muddy and bedraggled, the dogs mouth was still open in a grin and his tail waved proudly.

Shiloh turned, the corner of his mouth quirking up a notch beneath his beard. "Hey there, Miss Tanner. How you holding up in this lovely weather?"

"As well as could be expected." Ami suddenly wished very hard for a lovely dress, a darling hat, and a decent updo. *But really, I'd settle to be dry.*

"You'll be glad to know, I heard Captain Reckon say we'll be stopping here until the rain passes and the ground dries up a bit. Some of the lesser wagons are creaking awfully bad, and he doesn't want anyone to lose a wheel."

"Oh, thank the Lord in Heaven." A grin broke out on Ami's face.

Shiloh bent toward her, and in a swift motion pushed a wet strand of hair back from her forehead. "You have a beautiful smile, you know that?" Just as quickly, he moved away and was gone.

Shiloh? Could he possibly fancy me? Ami was accustomed to thwarting all kinds of suiters, all the way from primary school days when Samuel Wilson gave her a bouquet of daisies that was home to a bee which had stung him in the nose. Since joining the wagon train, she'd become rather adept at evading the more serious advances of the single men, and a few of the married ones. But

Shiloh's eyes held something different. A spark of kindness, of care.

But he's no Paul Amos. Ami shook her head and skirted back behind the wagon to let the children know about the break.

9
The Slogging Times

Rain fell without end for another two days. Hard enough to soak everyone, but, thankfully, not so much as to flood the wagons off the trail. Ami began to think the constant drizzle and drip would never go away. Most of their time was spent huddled in the wagon around the sheet stove, nibbling on stale Johnnycake and provisions from the dried goods store.

The older children did their best to keep in good spirits, but little Heston had an earache, and he leaned against his mama most of the day, whimpering. The second day, Ami scooted off to Jerusha's wagon to beg a remedy. Jerusha sent her back full of tea and with an ointment that smelled like the very Devil himself. The vile concoction worked its magic, and Heston was his cheerful self a few hours later.

The afternoon of the fourth rainy day in a row, Captain Reckon announced the rain had lightened up enough for them to continue. "We're only a few hours from the banks of the Big Muddy at Plattsmouth. We'll be through Iowa tonight if we keep going."

A thin cheer rose from the crowd. Town meant shops, provisions, and maybe even a night at a boarding house for the privileged few who could afford it. They slogged through the mud, the goal of Nebraska and civilization as a beacon to move them forward.

Ami barely remembered pitching the tent and climbing into her sopping bed. Weariness had so overcome her soul that the dirt and the dank didn't matter a whit.

The merciful velvet of sleep, deep and dreamless, was all too short. She awoke with a start. Ellie stirred and opened her eyes.

"Hear that? Ami cupped a hand behind her ear.

"Birds singing," Ellie mumbled. "And a river rushing . . ."

"But no rain!" Ami squealed. They tumbled over each other like children to peek their heads out of the tent.

The sky blazed with the reds, golds and pinks of sunrise. But there wasn't a cloud in sight.

Martha was outside, coaxing up a fire from the precious dried wood they'd hoarded in the wagon. "The men are out hunting by the river. Hopefully we'll get fresh meat for stew, but if not, we can go to town and purchase new vittles. I could do with fresh bread and more sugar, how about you?"

"Fresh bread would be lovely, Mother." Ellie clasped her hands together.

"We'll be here for quite a while, at least the day," said Martha. "The wagons need a going over to check for repairs and they'll have to arrange for a ferry to get us across."

Francie waltzed into camp, somehow looking daisy-fresh despite the harrowing last few days. Ami fought back a pang of jealousy.

"Maggie and I are going into town. You can't imagine the things we can see and do there. Why, they have a steamship coming in this afternoon, wagon master told my father. And we'll be joining up with another group. They say the Indian problems are so bad we won't survive with just eighteen wagons."

"Another group? What other group?" Ami asked.

At this, Martha and Francie began to chuckle. Francie swept her hands out. "Look around you, silly."

Ami stood and stretched, surveying the vast fields between their wagon and the Platte River. "Oh, the rain was so thick yesterday, and I was so tired, I didn't even see them." Dozens, hundreds of schooners, stretched out as far as she could see. People milled around them in clumps, like tiny tin soldiers.

"Where did they all come from?" Ami breathed.

"They've been here, apparently," said Martha. "Many of the groups came from the Missouri route, the one we decided not to take. This is where they intersect. Captain Reckon is scouting for a group we can join. Bartholomew Hinkle's family is heading home on the steamboat, so that's two wagons we'll be losing. Their grandmother's ailing and they won't go on without her, plus Mrs. Hinkle is fearful with all this talk of the Indians being stirred up again."

"Do you think we should be worried, Mother?" Ellie's eyes were two round blue moons against her pale skin.

"Don't be silly." Francie patted her shoulder. "Like I said, we'll be joining up with another train, maybe two. No Indian can stand against us."

If we join with another group, we'll have to deal with more silly people and move even slower. Ami's shoulders sagged. *What could be worse?* She could be planning her wedding to Bernard Regent right now, that's what could be worse.

She made her way to the area where the stock had been tethered. Mister was busily tearing fresh grass from the ground, but as Ami approached, he raised his head, stalks hanging from his mouth.

"You greedy thing. Here's something you might like better." Ami pulled out an apple she'd smuggled from the provisions and held it out to him.

Mister took a few steps toward her and reached out for the fruit. He took it daintily as a lady at tea and began crunching it between his wide yellow teeth, the juice foaming around his mouth.

After gulping it down he nuzzled her dress, searching for more.

"Silly boy, that's all I have." Ami chuckled, but something nagged at her. Mister's steps had faltered, and he seemed to favor his left foreleg. She blinked. It had to be her imagination, but after all this rain, she'd better check his hooves.

She drew an ever-present hoof pick from her apron. Leaning against Mister, she tugged on the worrisome leg until he lifted it without protest. She'd been doing this with him since he was a newly broken colt.

As usual, small rocks and twigs were mixed in with the mud that always filled the hollow part of Mister's hoof. But everything seemed to be fine. No signs of swelling or heat from infection. Ami breathed a sigh of relief and dropped his leg back to the carpet of grass.

Mister gave her a look that seemed to say, "Can I get back to my breakfast now?" He dipped his head.

"Your inclination is right." Shiloh came up behind her. "The horse is lame. If you keep riding him, he'll be beyond help very soon. You must find somewhere for him to rest, and the trail isn't the place for that."

"I checked him just now, as you know, since your habit is to sneak up on people." Ami swallowed a lump forming in her throat.

"Sometimes these things hit without much warning," Shiloh said. He patted Mister's chestnut flank. "This horse wasn't bred for months of hard travel. Miss Tanner, you're a horse woman. I can tell by the way you ride. Whoever ran your daddy's stable was a fine hand, and he taught you right. But Mister shouldn't be on the trail." His voice grew softer, and a kindness entered his eyes she'd only seen that night when he'd held the Dawson baby. "I can see the thunder settled on your face. And I wouldn't hurt you for all the gold in California. I know it would plumb kill you to let Mister go, but you wouldn't want him to die, either, would you? I've lost animals that I loved, and I . . ."

Ami clenched her fists to her sides. "You make me sound like I'm some terrible lout, like that man who doesn't care properly for his ox. Like you said, I am a horsewoman, Mr. Talon, and I know the state of my beast. He's fine." These last two words were uttered as more of a hiss then she'd intended, even in her anger.

Shiloh held up his gloved hands. "Have it your way. If you change your mind, I've bought a spare mount in town this morning. See that Morgan over there? His name's Cavalry. Brought his last owner out of the battlefields of Virginia."

Ami followed his gesture and couldn't hold back a splutter of laughter. "That beast? His tail is as raggedy as the old blanket we have tacked up on the back of the wagon. And I don't know how he'd carry you, he's almost tiny enough to be a pony."

Shiloh's smile widened, which infuriated Ami even more. "I take it you've never seen a Morgan in action. Cavalry's a tough old coot, but he's a gentleman. I'm willing to wager he could beat any horse here in a test of endurance, and probably outpull some of the mules."

Ami freed Mister's tether and dug around the peg to loosen it from the ground. "I don't intend to discuss this any further, and I certainly don't want that scarecrow of a horse, Mr. Talon. I'd prefer not to have this conversation again. You do understand."

"Perfectly." Shiloh gave her the infuriating grin once more and walked off, his dog at his heels.

"Oooh." Ami stomped her foot and immediately regretted the gesture. She hoped Shiloh hadn't seen the childish movement. *He already treats me like a child.* But then she gulped, remembering the tender way he'd pushed her hair back during the rain and the concern in his eyes when he'd warned her about the secret.

A thought tickled the back of her mind, like a tiny pebble rolling around a large stone urn. *What if he's right? What if Mister is going lame?* The rain wasn't good for any of the stock.

Mister tossed his head and snorted. Despite being covered with dried mud and Ami not having a chance to curry him, he was still a magnificent creature.

Hogwash in the barn. That Shiloh Talon doesn't know what he's talking about. Mister could travel the Oregon trail three times over and still take me to church on Sunday.

Shiloh sat on the outskirts of camp, away from most of the clustered families but close enough to hear what Reckon had to say. The wagon leader had called a full meeting that night.

Firelight flickered from pits dotting the banks, dug out by wagon goers from decades past.

Reckon stood in the middle, his chest puffed up and chin jutted out. Disdain bubbled up inside of Shiloh's chest. How many times had the wagon master decided not to heed his advice and warnings? It was only by God's grace a more serious accident had not befallen the party. Shiloh stared at his hands. *I'll keep silent this time. If the man falters, it's on him.*

Reckon gestured to a burly man with a thick black beard who stood beside him. "This is Captain Marshall. He's leading a party of thirty-five wagons from Independence. They were two days ahead of us until the rain, so perhaps they can help you all learn faster methods of travel." He raised a thick eyebrow and glared at a few men Shiloh knew to be lazier than the others. "You will speak to Captain Marshall as you would address me. As many of you know, the United States government has made it mandatory that all wagon trains from here on out be comprised of forty wagons or more. Thirty-five extra wagons with men and guns will assuredly protect us through Indian territory. We have heard rumors of massacres. Let me promise you, they are true. Captain Marshall?" He gestured again, and the burly man stepped forward.

Angry spots flickered past Shiloh's eyes. As a scout, this matter of joining the Marshall train should have been discussed with him and Joe Loggins. But Reckon hadn't even bothered to introduce them. The flippant disrespect he'd been given piled up to a peak and crashed down around his ears. He set his jaw. *I'll join a different team. Plenty around here to choose from.*

But then he caught sight of a peach and purple bonnet, streaked with mud, bobbing among the crowd. He sighed. *Ami will never make it to Oregon with that horse of hers. Someone must be there for her when Mister falters.* Though to his credit, Mister had lasted over a month when he'd given him a week at the beginning. But the horse was faltering. *Ami knows it, she just can't admit it yet.*

"We are happy to be of service to your company," Mr. Marshall's booming voice broke through his thoughts. "Another group has felt the sad loss from the fierce tribes to the west only this month. Two men grew impatient and crossed the Platte in their wagon alone. Word returned that their wagon was found stripped of all worth, their animals butchered, and the two poor fellows killed and scalped."

A few of the woman covered their eyes, and every man's face sobered. Shiloh's fingers clenched into fists. He'd heard this very story many times on different legs of the trail. A common tale used to keep wagon trains banded together. While the danger of attacks from hostiles were real, there was no sense making up tales.

Mr. Marshall continued. "But there's nothing to fear. The Indians won't attack a group this large, leastways if we all stay together, and shoot the red men on sight."

Shiloh stepped forward, his moccasins barely making a whisper on the brittle earth. His stomach twisted like he'd eaten bad berries, and he fought to keep his voice level. "No need to shoot on sight, Captain Marshall, and I think Captain Reckon will agree with me. This isn't my first venture west. Hundreds of natives live in peaceful settlements along the trail. Most who'd have hostile intent stay out of sight. You wouldn't even know they're watching you until your horses are miles away."

"Or you've been scalped." Mr. Marshall said dryly. "Keep to your business, boy. We'll let you know if we need your opinion."

Shiloh caught Jerusha's eye from where she sat across the fire. She sucked in a breath and shook her head.

Shiloh tipped his hat. "Deepest pardons, sir, but I was hired on to help scout for this train, and I thought you'd want the input of someone who's walked the path. There's no sense in murdering random folks and making an enemy of someone who doesn't have to be."

Mutterings of agreement and dissent rose up from the crowd.

Reckon gave Shiloh a slanted glance. He scuffed the dirt with the toe of a boot but did not speak.

Shiloh clenched his jaw to hold back angry words that would most likely start a fireside brawl. He could tell Reckon agreed with him, but he wanted to 'play nice' with Captain Marshall.

Shiloh stepped back to his fireside corner and bowed his head. *I can't change the hearts of men, God. But I can do my best to keep the peace. If there's a way, please show me.*

10
Crossing the Platte

The stench of mold filled the air. Blankets, tents and clothing were washed multiple times in the river and laid out on any flat surface to dry in the welcome sunshine.

A few items were declared impossible to salvage and had to be replaced. Fortunately, the frugal Martha had been informed of this possibility by her husband and was prepared for the inflated prices of the supplies offered in the river town.

Ami was more grateful now than ever for the scented soap, which helped mask the musky, moldy smell that permeated everything.

After two days of repairs and preparation, the people of both wagon trains declared their wagons and stock ready to cross. Many of the wagons could be rolled right on to the gigantic ferry raft and floated over.

Francie and Ami rode to the river's edge to watch the wagons as they were loaded. This was considered man's work, and it seemed a back-breaking, sweaty, dangerous job. Ami was happy not to be a part of it.

"Papa said in the days before the ferry was made, they'd have to take the wagon wheels off and float the wagons like boats," said Francie, fanning herself with a lady's magazine she'd purchased in town.

Ami groaned. A task like that would take forever to prepare for.

Most of the stock were loaded on to the second ferry just fine, but a few of the oxen lowered their heads, bellowed, and stamped their giant cloven hoofs.

These animals would have to be tied to the back of the ferry by leads and swum across. Still a much less dangerous venture than the 'olden days,' as Francie called them. "Why, they sometimes lost two or three men a day." Her pretty green eyes widened. "They'd be caught in the current and washed up on shore, dead as June bugs!"

The actual crossing was much less dramatic. After the wagons and oxen made it to shore, the women and children took the next turn. Martha and Ellie herded the children on board, while Ami rode Mister up with Francie and Thaddeus and their horses. They stayed mounted all the way across, watching the peaceful ripples of the quieted river. Mister stayed placid, as though he rode ferries across bodies of water every day of his life.

"I heard we were lucky to get the rain," Thaddeus remarked. "Sometimes the Platt's too low to handle the ferries. Then the trains have to go several miles downstream or try to slog across through the mud."

"I had no idea we faced such varying circumstances," said Ami. "But hopefully the rain will let up for a time at least, since this is the only major river crossing for some time."

They reached the other side. As Ami dismounted and began to lead Mister off the ship, she noticed a slip in his step. Her heart leapt to her throat, and blood began pounding in her head. *No, no, Mister. Please don't let Shiloh be right. I can't lose you.*

She rubbed him down carefully and gave him an extra measure of oats. *Maybe he's just a bit seasick.*

Exhausted from the day's efforts, the immigrants made camp a mile from the Platte's shore. The air was filled with dust and the frustrated shouts of men. Children and women held the lead shanks of animals while the wagon-masters argued over how to position three times as many wagons as they had been accustomed to organizing.

When it was all over and supper fires were finally lit, Ami wandered off to a quiet rock by the river. She buried her head in her arms, listening to the mournful cries of whippoorwills in the trees, and, more alarmingly, the far-off scream of a panther.

"Been a rough day, huh?" Shiloh plopped down beside her and stretched out on the ground, leaning against the log she'd chosen.

Ami nodded and rested her chin in her hands. "I wonder if this is all worth it. I've heard Oregon is a beautiful land, with crops that grow by just throwing seeds into the ground and leaving them. But what do I know about crops? What am I even doing here? And Mister." A lump bubbled into her throat, and she didn't dare speak for fear of bursting into tears. She closed her eyes. *Mister, Mister, Mister! What have I done to you!*

"Hey." Shiloh sat up and brushed her chin, just barely, with the tip of his finger. "I'll help you find a good home for your horse. A family I know runs a boarding house in the next town, most wagon trains stop there. They have a large bath house and offer decent food. I'll talk to the man if you like. If they don't buy Mister, he'll know someone who will. They're good people and will care for Mister like he was one of their children."

Suddenly it was all too real for Ami. She was truly going to have to give up her horse. Unable to hold back hot tears, she allowed them to drip off the edge of her nose in a most unbecoming fashion. "My mother gave him to me. He's the only thing I have left." She could barely make out the next words. "I would be such a disappointment to her."

"I don't know why you left your home," Shiloh said softly. "But I'm sure it was for a good reason. Your mother would be proud of the strong daughter she raised."

Ami wasn't quite sure how it all happened, but all at once Shiloh had folded her in his arms, with her head resting on his shoulder. At any other time she would have been scandalized and worried that someone from camp would happen upon her spot by the water, but at this moment, she didn't care. Comfort and peace coursed through her soul, and she stayed in his arms for what seemed like eternity, until the dinner bell rang and pulled them from the little castle they'd built in time.

Shiloh stomped along the thin path, well aware his movements would scare away any of the game he intended to hunt. A pheasant started up before him in a flurry of wings. Shadow barked profusely, then tipped his head to the side.

Thaddeus chuckled behind him. "Yes, Shadow, I'm wondering the same thing about your master. Shiloh, what's gotten into you? Everyone's craving a bit of venison, but we're never going to catch a thing at this rate."

Shiloh's shoulders slumped. "Sorry. Too much on my mind, I guess. I'm worried about Indian encounters. That Marshall has everyone scared as rabbits. The guards are liable to shoot a member of the train if they're not careful."

Thaddeus grimaced. "We're all God's creatures, no matter what blood courses through our veins. When I was young, I dreamed of being a missionary to the Indians like the great Dr. Whitman. I believe in protecting our own, but innocent blood should never be shed out of needless fear."

"That's what I'm saying," Shiloh folded his arms. "I've met a great number of these people. They want to trade and make money off the trains, sure. Many of them simply want to be left in peace. Was a time when Indians were considered so worthless settlers would shoot them on site, as Captain Marshall suggested, as though they were a trophy or something."

"So tragic." Thaddeus shook his head.

"I've seen what Indians can do as well." Shiloh swiped at the grass with a long stick he was carrying. "There are good folks and bad folks of every type."

Thaddeus sighed. "Hard to believe anyone with a soul could treat another in that fashion."

"Not much different than thinking one man has a right to own another," Shiloh said.

"True. I only wish I had been old enough to join the war when the call was given," Thaddeus replied.

Shiloh studied the earnest face of the young man beside him. "Be thankful you didn't, and find other ways to fight injustice," he said firmly.

The two friends trudged in silence for a spell.

No animal sounds could be heard, and the scats and tracks were all at least a day old. "Maybe we should try our hand at fishing," said Shiloh."

"Hmm." Thaddeus pursed his lips. "I think I know what's really bothering you. Could it have something to do with a lady who wears a certain orange and purple bonnet?"

Shiloh stopped short and dropped his stick.

"There's no sense in denying it." Thaddeus continued. "I don't blame you. Miss Tanner is a beautiful woman, and strong of character." His tone was kind, not mocking, but his words still buzzed like annoying bees in Shiloh's ears.

"Look, I might have a bit of an attachment to her, but that doesn't change anything. Even if she had feelings for me . . . we aren't equals. You can see who she is." Shiloh spread out his hands. "And you know who I am. We aren't meant to be."

Thaddeus pushed a branch out of the way so they could pass through. "Seems to me like the trail has made you equals. Sure, she's a fine lady, used to fine things. But she slogs through the mud like the rest of us. Like I said before, I believe we're all equals in the sight of the Almighty." He shrugged. "Look at us. My family has riches beyond most of these folks' wildest dreams but money only gets us so far out here. We can't pay the rain away, or for a steep hill to smooth itself. I'd give all the money we possess to stop somewhere and settle. Trail life isn't for me."

"Me either," Shiloh said absentmindedly.

Thaddeus's mouth dropped open. "But you're a scout. Isn't that your job?"

"Not after this trip. When I reach Oregon this time, I'm going to stay. I'm ready to give up schooner life."

"All the more so if Miss Tanner happens to settle in the general vicinity?" asked Thaddeus.

Shiloh paused and rubbed his chin. "Perhaps."

11
Moving On

Sludge covered the trail once more, due to rain from the previous evening. Ami lagged behind the schooners, close enough to stay in earshot but far enough to have her own space. Francie had invited her to the Herschel family wagon to partake in a box of sweetmeats she'd purchased in the river town, but Ami knew anything she ate today would stick in her throat.

Five gold coins had been added to the purse she kept around her neck most of the time, but it seemed like the weight of a noose.

Cavalry's steps were solid and sure through the mud. His tattered ears swiveled back and forth, and he always seemed poised and alert, ready for any enemy or danger. To Ami, he seemed more dog than horse. Her heart hurt too much to admit it, but Shiloh was right. Cavalry was much better suited for the trail.

The innkeeper's eyes had lit up when he'd seen Mister, and he'd given a low whistle. "He's a beautiful creature, and there's no mistake about it. We'll get him fixed up in no time. He'll be the perfect horse for my wife."

There'd been slight comfort in knowing Mister would continue to be a lady's horse. He'd be pampered and loved by the boarding house couple.

Shiloh had been so kind to her. He'd found her in the barn, sobbing her heart out. He'd held her close and stroked her hair without saying a word. And he'd known the right time to leave her alone with Mister for her last goodbye.

Mister watched her with those beautiful wise eyes. "Oh Mister." She kissed his soft nose. "I'm so sorry I did this to you. I should've never dragged you out here to this place. What was I thinking?" Fresh tears fell once more, though she'd thought all the water in her body would be gone by now. "I'm so selfish. Why couldn't I have just married Bernard? I'd have to live with the most repugnant man imaginable, but then I'd never need to part with you."

She'd slept at the boardinghouse the night before. The luxury of a real bed and hot bath had been ruined by the knowledge that this moment was coming. The night had been a sleepless one, where she'd gone over the last five weeks, the hasty decision brought on by a spurt of temper. Her father always said her temper would be her downfall. She hated to admit it, but this time it was hard to deny.

Mister whiffed in her ear with little whistling sighs, like he always did when she was sad. She'd always felt like he comprehended everything she told him. But as she hugged him one last time, and breathed in his horsey scent, she knew he'd never understand why she left.

When she walked out of the barn, he'd whinnied long and loud, louder than she'd ever heard him.

Shiloh was waiting for her outside. "Miss Tanner, we must leave. Almost everyone who spent the night is back at camp."

"Hear him?" she sobbed once more. "He knows. He knows I'm leaving him."

Shiloh took her hand and swung her around gently to face him. "Look, Ami, I'm so terribly sorry. But . . . I wanted to tell you. If you need to go home, I'll take you there. I'm not sure how we'll make it, but we'll figure something out."

She pulled out a pocket handkerchief and scrubbed her eyes. Shiloh stood there so sincere and kind, the morning sun lighting his tousled head. It was enough to start her sobbing again, but she swallowed hard instead. "It's terribly kind of you, Shiloh. The kindest thing anyone's ever offered me. But I can't go back. Nothing waits for me but a life of misery. If I continue forward on this journey, there's always a chance . . . for something more."

His jaw relaxed, and he smiled. "All right then, Miss Tanner. Let's continue on our way, and we'll pray God breathes favor over us."

The wagon train had been on the move for three days now since that fateful morning. *Mister will never forgive me.* Ami's lip trembled. *I should have begged the boarding-house owner for a job and stayed with them.*

But what future could there be for a lady with no training in cooking and cleaning? She'd only had a month's worth of experience on the trail in which she'd barely learned how to scorch Johnnycake. Martha left her with the tasks of minding children or repairing canvas wagon covers and tents, while Martha and Ellie generally took on more of the household duties.

These thoughts rolled through Ami's mind like distasteful foods over her tongue, which led to more uncomfortable notions, the ones she'd tried to stuff down like clothes in an overflowing trunk. What would she do when she reached Oregon? How would she support herself? She couldn't count on the charity of strangers, and Martha would have her hands full keeping her own flesh and blood alive. With two older boys waiting at their homestead, she would no longer require Ami's help.

Paul Amos. His face floated into her mind for the first time in weeks. She'd been so much younger, that night she'd spent dreaming of a stranger. Now the absurdity of her silly plan to maybe find one man in the whole state of Oregon chafed at her soul as badly as her leather shoes rubbed at her ankles when they were wet from the rain.

Paul might not end up in Oregon. Many of the folks from the new wagon train had discussed the benefits of branching off to

Montana instead. It was several weeks closer, and everyone was ready to be done with this journey, though they weren't even halfway to their destination. Some folks discussed California as an option. Though Oregon had always been the promised land, the days of rain followed by the difficult river crossing had been a bitter cup to swallow.

Amazingly, Francie Herschel had stayed cheerful. Ami heard her now, through the trees. "Maggie, stop dawdling! We must keep up with the wagons."

"The wagons are so much slower than they used to be," came Maggie's slightly whiny voice. "I plan to finish gathering these berries for Mama. You know how she loves them."

Ami rolled her eyes and urged Cavalry further into the thicket towards the girls' voices.

Cavalry tossed his absurdly tiny, though nicely shaped head and snorted. She'd quickly realized the ex-war horse disliked moving through thick brush, presumably because an enemy could ambush him at any time.

"You need to learn some manners," she murmured, and tapped him with her heels. He moved forward in sulking steps.

By the time she reached Maggie and Francie, the two girls were facing each other with crossed arms and sullen scowls. She slipped off Cavalry and approached them.

"Hello, Ami," Francie smiled, though she continued to glare at her sister. "How's your new horse working out for you? I was so sorry to hear about Mister."

Ami hesitated. She wondered if Francie was being sincere, as she'd often made slightly jealous comments about Mister. *Im going spend at least two months more on the trail with her, and she's pretty much the only friend I have.* She shrugged. "Cavalry will do. I'm fortunate Shiloh sold him to me. No one's had a good horse for sale in the last two towns."

"You're lucky Shiloh's sweet on you." Maggie blinked at Ami, her eyes innocent and wide. "My papa said that horse was worth twice what you paid for him."

Ami glowered but didn't say anything. *I shouldn't have told them how much I paid. Teaches me to let my personal business slip.*

"Maggie, we need to get going now." Francie snatched her sister's berry basket from where it sat on a log. "Mama said we can't stay too far behind. Do you want to be scalped or taken as an Indian's slave?"

"Indians aren't all bad." Shiloh strode through the trees. "In fact, a group of them saved my life a few years ago. I'd taken a job scouting with a wagon train headed to California and they dawdled too long, just like the Donner party. I went out hunting and got stuck in a snowstorm in Colorado. Group of Utes took me in and sheltered me for the whole winter. I couldn't be more grateful. My father was a soldier and my family lived near a fort in Texas, so we dealt with natives, friendly and not so friendly, all the time. Indian children were my closest friends growing up."

Francie shuddered. "How could you stand being with such dirty, uncivilized creatures?"

Shiloh gave his lopsided smile. "They would wonder how you could wear such a flowery scent to scare away the prey for miles. Each tribe has their own laws and rules to abide by. It's us that's disrupted them."

Shiloh whistled, and his dog bounded from the forest, cockleburs sticking in his fur.

"Shadow, you scamp. Let's get you back to the river so I can pull those out." He glanced up at the ladies. "Though I'm a friend to most natives and will defend them to the teeth, I agree with your mama, Maggie. You should stay close to the wagons. It's not only Indians who might attack. There are plenty of white folks with evil in their hearts. Raiders and bandits are often encountered throughout the trail. They're most likely to show up in places like these, farther from towns and sheriffs. Can you please be more careful?"

Maggie huffed, but nodded.

As Francie and Maggie headed back to camp, Shiloh spoke softly to Ami. "Actually, I've been meaning to mention this. I'm worried for you. I don't like how some of the men from the new wagon train watch you."

"For Pete's sake, Shiloh!" Ami snapped. "I know how to deal with men and their advances. I've about smacked Captain Reckon more than once, and some of your beloved teamsters too. Leave me be, it's not like I belong to you."

Shiloh flinched as though she'd slapped him and a rare flush crept over his cheeks. "I would never imply that, but I've learned how to read men pretty well. A few trips back, a woman who lost her husband was–treated with impropriety. She almost died." He suddenly gripped her shoulder. "I want you to be safe. Please watch yourself."

Ami started to pull away, but the look in his eye was sincere and intense.

"I will," she murmured.

"Good," he said. "I care about . . . everyone in our wagon train. It's my job to keep all of you safe, and I'm determined to see it through to the end." His shoulders slumped. "As hard as our leaders make that sometimes."

Is that all? Does he only care because it's his job? Ami shook her head. She'd spent the last several years learning to understand men and their intentions. The look in Shiloh's eyes, and the interactions they'd had lately, especially the one a few nights ago by the lake, didn't line up with his words. *Why is he being so cautious? Is he afraid of rejection?* But Shiloh Talon didn't seem to be a man of fear in any sense. *Would I reject him?*

The question made her chuckle a bit. Was there any question? Of course she couldn't be with a man like Shiloh. He knew nothing of gentry, of formality.

A pang of remorse hit her between the eyes. That was the old Ami's thoughts. Shiloh treated folks with care and dignity, which was more than she could say for most of the people she'd been surrounded by in her daily life. In fact, most of the folks from their original wagon train treated each other with kindness and friendship. There were no people of higher status even though the Herschel family sometimes pretended to be. Everyone worked side by side, as equals.

###

That evening Ami sat in Jerusha's wagon, helping the old woman tear blankets into strips for bandages.

Jerusha wiped sweat from her forehead. "It seems we go through dozens of these a day. The men come to me with cuts and scrapes from dealing with stock, and women and children have burns and every other ailment you can imagine." She glanced over at her little shelf of jarred, labeled remedies that was lashed to the wall to prevent breakage. "Mr. Granbury had a nasty gash from that ox he's had trouble with. I was tempted to turn him away. I can't abide a man who mistreats his animals."

Ami bowed her head. "Me either."

Jerusha shook out a raggedy sheet and held it up. "Instead I made him let me treat the ox first. And was he mad!" She sighed. "I'm afraid my ministrations won't do much good. That poor ox is a walking skeleton. I'm amazed it's lasted this long."

"Poor thing," said Ami.

"But we all must do our part to help others." Jerusha tore the sheet down the middle, then began to tear one half into smaller strips. "Especially as the wagon train has grown so. Do you know Captain Marshall's group has two women who are expecting babies?"

Ami gasped. "When will they be born?"

"Probably before we reach Oregon." Jerusha rolled another bandage and placed it on the snowy stack they'd built. "Why any woman would choose to give birth along the trail is beyond my comprehension." She tugged another cloth from the rag basket at her feet. "I've already gone 'round to tell them of my services. They were mighty grateful to know, and so were their husbands."

"I'm sure," Ami murmured.

"The other group has a doctor. A man," Jerusha said scornfully. "He might know how to stitch up a cut, but I'd bet he doesn't know how to bring a baby onto this earth. And that's the truth. What would those women have done if I hadn't come along?" There was no pride in Jerusha's voice, just incredulousness.

Ami's cheeks burned at the subject, though she had begun to expect such topics from Jerusha. "Babies come into the world, no matter what," she said. "But you think the menfolk would have more compassion. They could go to Oregon the year after, perhaps."

"Not just the menfolk." Jerusha said. "Other mamas and grandmas can possess little care and regard as well. It's like memories of their time fly right out of their head and they expect those new mothers to get right up and shovel out a barn of manure.

More women I've seen die from sepsis or fatigue than you can imagine."

Ami placed the last bandage on a pile. "I guess I never thought about that. Ladies in my circle were shut away from the world on bedrest for weeks and weeks after they had babies. No one talked to them or about them. If anyone mentioned the time, it was called a 'confinement.'"

Jerusha picked up the basket of bandages and shut them away in a little cupboard. "That can be just as bad. It's important to get up and move around, get the body going again. Fresh sunshine for mama and child."

"I hope to have someone like you close by if I ever have children," said Ami. "Though at this point, I'll probably end up an old maid." The moment she'd said the words, she wished to snatch them back from the air. She covered her mouth. "I mean . . . I didn't mean . . ."

Jerusha chuckled. "What makes you think I'm an old maid? No, I'm just an old widow. I had my love, Zebedee, and lost him at twenty-five years of age. We experienced seven wonderful years of life and I never wanted another fellow." She paused, giving Ami an appraising look. "You're a sweet, smart, lovely girl. I very strongly doubt you'll be an old maid either, though there are worse things to be in this world."

Ami remembered the look in Shiloh's eye when he'd been talking about the wagon train and caring for the people on it. She was starting to recognize that glint and had a sneaking suspicion it was for her.

12
Sparks

Ami awoke to a ruckus outside of her tent. She poked her head out to see men running everywhere, and women clutching their children close, peeking through canvas covers. Martha stood close to the wagon, a deep furrow formed over her forehead.

Ami sniffed the air. *No smoke. That's good, at least.*

"What's going on?" Ami asked Martha.

Martha turned and shrugged. "Seems seven of the oxen went missing in the night."

Ami's hand flew to her mouth. "Ours?"

Martha sighed. "Are safe. No wild animal tracks were seen, so they think it's Indians. Six of the oxen belonged to Mr. Granbury."

Despite the gravity of the situation, Ami couldn't help but grin. "Serves him right." She stepped out of the wagon and stretched her legs. "Maybe the Indians will treat those poor beasts better than he did."

"I'd say you're wicked for thinking such a thing," Martha poked at a seam in the canvas that was coming undone. "But in this case, you're right. Man's getting what he deserves. However, out here stock animals like that are nearly impossible to replace. He'll be forced to turn back or wait in the next town until he can buy more oxen."

"You mean we won't have the Granbury's wagon behind us anymore?" Ami clasped her hands in front of her.

Martha leaned over and spoke just above a whisper. "Quiet now, he might hear you! It's unlucky to speak ill of those with bad fortune, but in this case I'm glad to be rid of such an evil-tempered man. We must keep better watch of the stock. We can't be losing any of our animals." She wiped sweat of her forehead with an apron corner. "Even losing one beast right now would be terrible for us. We still have at least eight weeks to go, that's what Captain Reckon has been telling us. I thought for sure having more people in our group would keep us safe."

"Maybe the oxen wandered off. Couldn't we send out a search party?" Ami asked.

"That's what Shiloh said. He's certain Mr. Granbury didn't secure his stock correctly. Warned him about it several times. But the captains aren't having it." Martha moved over to the campfire and stirred the eternal pot of bubbling porridge with a stick. "They said it's too likely the men will get caught out in small groups and scalped . . . and then the natives might come back here and finish everyone else off." She shuddered.

"Do you really think we're in that much danger?"

Martha tapped her chin. "I've heard most of the tribes are moving away from the trail, especially after the war. And the natives my husband encountered on his journey were friendly. They'd either trade with the groups or keep to themselves, just like Shiloh said. My husband wouldn't have asked me to come if he didn't think God would keep us safe. I have to trust that. But you hear the stories."

Ami moved along the side of the wagon, scanning the thick canvas for tears and weakened spots. A part of her knew good men existed in this world, men who cared for their wives and children, but after her father had betrayed her and chosen Millany over his own daughter, it was hard to believe sometimes. Even Shiloh's kindness could be explained away. *If he fancies me.*

She threaded a thick needle she always kept in her pocket and jabbed it through the canvas, pulling two frayed edges together. The tiniest tear could turn into a giant problem, and the canvas patches they kept rolled up under the wagon were small and few. They'd already given several pieces to other wagon owners.

There. The torn place was mended. She stepped back to admire her work. They were a far cry from the delicate stitches her mother had tried so patiently to teach her from five years old and on, but much more practical.

Even now, her old life seemed like such a distant memory, full of trivial and useless tasks. To think she'd spent half an hour discussing china pattern choices with Millany when the mayor's wife came to tea. That wasn't even the silliest thing. Ballgowns and hats and the proper number of petticoats. Some of the women on the trail only wore one. Some of them had never owned a corset. And they seemed fine. In fact, most of them were stronger, better women than she was. Sometimes she felt like a complete and useless oaf. The only saving grace she possessed was her knack with horses. She'd even earned a grudging respect with the men. No one else but Shiloh could ride Cavalry. The horse wouldn't let another person approach him, and yet with her, he was gentle as a kitten. *But it doesn't make me like him anymore.*

###

Another somber night. Folks spoke in low voices and moved quietly about their respective fires. At any sudden noise, men's fingers would fly to the blades on their hips or the guns by their sides.

A middle-aged couple from the other wagon train huddled together on a log, speaking in low voices. Ami assumed they were married, though with their matching matted salt and pepper hair and unkempt, sallow faces, they could be related. She'd noticed them both staring at her often, and each time she'd gulp back a lecture on manners.

Mrs. Granbury, a pale, slender woman who Francie said would almost disappear when she turned sideways, sat across from Ami, hands folded in her lap, vacant eyes staring into the darkened prairie. *If her husband treats beasts so terribly, how does he treat his wife?* Ami shuddered.

Ami had never experienced such a quiet as enveloped the camp that night. Even after the Dawson fire, people still joked and whistled snatches of songs to keep their spirits high. This night folks barely spoke above whispers, as though an avalanche of bad fortune could be unleashed at any moment, simply by the power of an uttered word.

"God, please help us," Ami whispered. "We can't go on in this fear. It will swallow us whole."

"This is no good." Shiloh came up beside Ami, so stealthily she jumped. "A camp of nervous folks are dangers to themselves. Someone's liable to get hurt."

Thaddeus sat down beside Shiloh. He rested his fiddle on his shoulder, closed his eyes, and drew the bow across the strings. A warbling hymn, sweet and somber, drifted through the night air and up to the stars.

Ami's chin sank to her chest. She recognized the song from church back home. The melody was beautiful, but the words were all about sorrow and suffering and marching on through the strife.

She felt Shiloh's eyes resting on her. He gave her a little nudge. "You all right, there, Miss Tanner?"

She nodded numbly. "I'm fine. The song makes me a little sad, I suppose."

Shiloh tapped Thaddeus on the shoulder. "Hey, Mr. Pious. We don't doubt your love for our great Lord in Heaven, but He created laughter as well as sorrow. Don't you think these folks could use a dose of happiness tonight?"

Thaddeus put his bow down and stared at Shiloh. "I suppose," he said slowly.

He plied his bow again, and this time a lively tune jumped from the strings, a melody filled with life and joy, color and strength.

"Come on, Miss Tanner, let's dance." Shiloh pulled at her hand.

"Dance?" Ami glanced at the faces, shadowed by firelight. "What will everyone think? And look at the ground! Riddled with rocks and holes. I'll turn my ankle and then you'll have to shoot me and leave me behind on the trail."

"Haven't you figured it out yet?" Shiloh stood and drew her after him. His breath was warm on her cheek. "I don't care what anyone else thinks." He whirled her around and pulled her close again. "And you know what else? I don't think you do either."

The next moment Ami was whirling and dancing, steps she'd never learned, but in which Shiloh led her as confidently as if he were tracking a deer or blazing a trail. Someone added a log to their fire, and sparks flew out and floated in the hazy air. Ami was vaguely aware of other dancers: Francie flew by on the arm of a gentleman from the other train, and Ami was almost certain she caught sight of Captain Marshall dancing a jig with Jerusha. Children jumped and twirled in the air, and dogs barked and ran in and out of the fray.

It's finally happened, the trail has made us all mad in the head. But if madness meant feeling this joy, this absolute freedom and abandonment, then maybe it was worth losing one's mind.

Finally, when she thought her lungs would burst, the music slowed again. Not to the former melancholy tune, but to a dreamy, heavenly piece that made her think of fairyland. Because she'd stopped questioning herself by now, she rested her head on Shiloh's shoulder and continued to follow his smooth, gliding steps. *This is where I belong. This is where I need to be. One wish. All I want. To dance by this fire forever, even if I never see a crumble of Oregon soil.*

As the first song slowed, Captain Reckon came behind Shiloh and tapped him on the shoulder. "Let me step in."

Ami had learned the rules of dance etiquette almost as soon as she'd learned to talk, and she knew that to decline was simply the rudest thing one could do. *Besides, what can one dance hurt?* She reluctantly stepped into a waltz with Captain Reckon. If the clumsy pattern he led her with could be called a waltz. Her feet were trodden upon almost instantly and she felt very inclined to lead as the man obviously had no notion of what he was supposed to do.

The older man pulled her close, his chest heaving with the effort. "Lovely night, Miss Tanner," he wheezed, the odor of rotten teeth wafting on his words.

"It is. Quite." Ami tried to turn her head enough to avoid the worst of the stench without seeming obvious.

"You know, I could make this trip much easier for you," Captain Reckon said in her ear. "Everyone knows you're a lady, more accustomed to finer things. I have connections in most of the towns from here on. We could come to a sort of arrangement. No one would need to know."

Ami pushed back away from him, white-hot anger blazing through her. "I'm fine where I'm at," she said, trying to keep an even tone so as not to attract more attention than she knew they would already be receiving.

He yanked her close again. "I'm sure you think you are, you and your scout," he said between clenched teeth. "But I'd advise you to watch yourself, Miss Tanner. A Train Captain is not the best person to have for an enemy."

Ami gave Thaddeus a wide-eyed look as they flew by. Thaddeus sent his bow to the end of the song a few stanzas short, and she stumbled away from Captain Reckon's angry face, back to the waiting arms of Shiloh.

"If someone else taps you on the shoulder. . . pretend you don't feel it," Ami murmured.

Shiloh grimaced. "Best plan anyone's had all day."

After many songs and much dancing, the evening came to a halt and most folks began to wander off to tents and wagons.

Shiloh squeezed Ami's hand. "You are a delightful dance partner, Miss Tanner, but I'm up for the first watch tonight. I must bid you farewell."

His formal words were in such contrast to his wild dress and nature that Ami held back a giggle. "The pleasure was all mine," she said, bobbing a tiny curtsey.

As Shiloh walked away from the fire, Ami sank down on a log beside Thaddeus. Ellie sat a few feet away, staring into the fire, her hands clasped in her lap.

"Thank you for the music tonight, Thaddeus," said Ami. "You know the hymns so well. I've never heard them played on the fiddle like that."

Thaddeus gave her a shy smile. "Always wanted to be a preacher. Felt the call of God on my life since I was ten years old. But my father's a banker, and since I'm the son, he's wanted me in the business. Money is the root of all kinds of evil." He glanced up at Ami with clear blue eyes. "That type of work just isn't for me. Father's a good man, but I've seen it change him. And that's not what I want for my life." He picked up his fiddle and ran his hand along the side. "When I play my violin, I feel like I'm right there in Heaven in the throne room of God. I know He hears me, and it pleases Him, because I'm doing it in reverence."

Ami twisted her hands in her lap. She'd never heard a man speak of God in such a way and wondered if it was blasphemous. To talk like God was among people, here on Earth, instead of up in the Heavens doing, well, Godly things. However, the rare times she saw Thaddeus in repose he was usually reading his Bible. He probably read more than the few fumbling verses she read by candlelight on mornings when she remembered. So maybe he was right. She'd certainly prayed more in the weeks since this trip had begun than she ever had in her life, at least since mama died.

She gave him a smile. "If God wills it for you, won't He help you make it come to pass?"

Thaddeus rubbed his chin. "I never thought about it that way. He is, after all, the Creator of the Universe. If he can build these amazing mountains surrounding us, he can surely accomplish the calling He's put on my life."

Ellie spoke up. "He will show you, Thaddeus. And you'll be the best preacher in Oregon. You'll see." The girl's cheeks bloomed crimson and she ducked her head.

"Thank you, Ellie." Thaddeus rose and picked up his fiddle. "I pray it will be so."

13
The Nez Perce

Dan and Dave, Martha's four and five-year-old sons, both stopped in the road, each with a berry halfway to their mouths. Despite the year's age difference, they were almost the same height and size, and both were so filthy that no one could tell one had blond hair and the other brown.

Ami's eyes followed their stares, and she froze, solid as a pond in a blizzard. Her heart pounded in her ears and she fought to steady herself.

A man stood on the edge of the trail. He wore the sort of breeches many of the farmers on the path possessed, and on his head was the same kind of floppy-brimmed hat that Shiloh sported. But that's where the similarities to any person she'd ever met ended. This man's features were etched in deep lines on dark umber skin. Two braids, woven with feathers and strips of rawhide, fell on either side of his head, and his vest was fashioned from beads and rows of polished porcupine quills. Most notably, a thin white bone ran through a hole in the center of his nose. He was wild, noble and beautiful, all at once. Ami bit her lip to keep from screaming, and the bitter metallic taste of blood brought her back to her senses. Every instinct told her to run, except a drop of common sense, which observed that the man carried no weapon, and could probably outrun her anyway. Instead she grabbed the boys and clutched them to her skirts.

"Hello?" she said tentatively.

"Hello." The man raised a hand.

Shiloh stepped out from the shadows. "Hey, there, Miss Tanner. Sorry if we gave you a fright, we didn't realize anyone would be out here on this part of the trail. Meet Ollicot of the Nez Perce tribe. I've encountered these folks twice on my other trips. The Nez Perce people are traders. They possess many useful things to help us on the rest of our journey."

"That's all well and good," Ami hissed, pulling Dave and Dan closer. "But what will Captain Reckon say? You know how spooked everyone is."

"Reckon knows of these folks as well as I do," said Shiloh. "The Nez Perce people have never been our enemies. They have no use for our livestock, for they hunt the buffalo, and their horses are far superior to even your Cavalry."

Ollicot spread out his arms. "I am a friend of Shiloh," he said. "Shiloh's woman is very pretty." He gave Ami a gleaming grin.

Shiloh fumbled with a buckle on his knife sheath. "Ollicot, I think you misunderstand. Miss Tanner's not my . . ." he glanced over at Ami. "Never mind."

Ami took a deep breath. "Nice to meet you, sir." She held out her hand.

Ollicot took it as gently, as though holding an injured bird. He pressed her fingers and let them go.

Dan, ever the outspoken one, wiggled out from Ami's grasp and stared up at Ollicot. "Are you going to scalp us?" he asked.

Ollicot smiled. "No, I only scalp very naughty children."

Dan scurried back to Ami, his eyes wide.

"He's joking with you, Danny," Ami whispered.

Shiloh watched, his lips twitching under his beard. "I suppose we'd better find Captain Reckon before some gun-happy settler sees us first."

The two men headed to the lead wagon.

Ami let out the breath she'd been holding in a long gusty exhale.

Dave tugged on her sleeve. "Aunt Ami, was that a good Indian? Mr. Granbury says the only good Indian is a dead one, but Mama says that's not true."

"No. Mr. Granbury is very wrong" Ami said, though when she spoke, she remembered the stories of massacres along the trail and her stomach twisted a little. "The world is full of evil people. Think of all the people who think it's right to own slaves and force them to do work for nothing."

Dave scowled. "Mama expects us to do work for nothing. Dan and I spend all the day collecting firewood."

Dan nodded. "All day," he echoed.

"Hmmm. Pretty sure I saw you two fishing by the river yesterday. And working together as a family isn't anywhere near the same as being a slave. Come on." Ami took their grimy hands into her own. "Let's see if your mama needs help with lunch."

That night Captain Reckon introduced Ollicot to the camp and allowed him to show samples of the brilliant blankets, beads and other items the tribe would have for trade. Captain Marshall stood to the side in glowering silence but did nothing to interfere.

A few settlers grumbled, but most were excited to see what the Nez Perce had to offer, since the next town was days away.

The group of eight Nez Perce people arrived in camp the next morning. Mostly men, but two women came as well, one with a bright-eyed baby strapped to her back. The women had flowing dark hair bound by beads and leather thongs and the same curious bones through their noses. They rolled out hides filled with bracelets, pottery and other handmade creations.

At first, the people from the wagon train were hesitant to approach the native people and their wares. But soon the men came closer to admire the thick, finely woven saddle blankets and women eyed the beautiful strings of beads and clay cooking pots.

Ami pulled a lace handkerchief from her valise and brought it to the woman with the baby. "Would you be interested in this?" she asked.

The woman gave her a broad smile and brushed the handkerchief with her fingertip. She wordlessly held up a long string of turquoise and green beads.

"Oh yes, perfect," Ami breathed. In her life, she'd owned boxes of what her father called 'fripperies,' pearls and combs and ribbons and trinkets, but never anything with the vivid colors in those beads. She wondered how the Nez Perce had created them.

"I'm Raven," the woman said. She gestured to the baby, who gurgled and cooed from the pack on her back. "This is Thomas."

"My name is Ami." Ami scooted around to admire the baby. "Your son is beautiful."

"Yes." Raven nodded. "He was born in the dawn, and the sun's first light touched his face. That is why he has such bright eyes."

Jerusha sat across from Ami and Raven, beside the other woman's blanket. Dried leaves and flowers were piled on a cloth in her lap.

"Are those for medicine?" Ami asked.

"Yes," said Jerusha. "And none too soon. I've run out of wandering milkweed, for skin ailments, and willow bark, which is a must for fever. Goodness knows I've had little time to gather it myself." She leaned closer to Ami. "Don't tell anyone where I get the remedies. Some of these folks would rather die as fools than take Indian medicine." She shook her head. "I'll never understand."

"Never, never!" Archibald squawked from her shoulder.

"Me either." Ami said. "My mother died of pneumonia. If I'd had a cure for her I wouldn't have cared where it came from."

Jerusha gestured to Shiloh, who was standing nearby. "Help an old woman up, will you?"

Shiloh held out an obliging hand. "I see you traded for slippery elm. Saved my life when I was a boy. An old Cherokee man brought it to our home after he heard I was sickened with influenza. It had already taken my big brother's life. He came just in time to save me and my father, too." He stroked Archibald's head, and the bird preened his feathers. "I'd forgotten that until now. That old man spent all day, spooning water and medicine down my throat a few drops at a time. He didn't know us from Adam."

So much tragedy for one man. And yet Shiloh seemed to have so much trust in God. *How can he hold on like that, when so many hard things have happened to him?* A new thought struck Ami. *Maybe it's because trust in God is all he has to hold onto.*

Ami picked up Jerusha's overflowing basket. "I'll help you with this." She waved to Shiloh. "See you soon."

Shiloh didn't glance her way. His eyes were trained on the trades going on in front of him. But he nodded. "Yes. Have a good day."

Ami followed Jerusha back to her wagon, which was, as usual, toward the end of the train. "How did you learn about cures and medicines?"

"My husband and I were missionaries to the Ottawa tribe in the 1830's, long before the country was torn by war." Jerusha brushed a strand of gray hair from her face. "The tribe had been moved from Iowa to Kansas, and many of them suffered great sicknesses. I knew very little about medicines, but I was allowed to work beside their healers. I think because they were desperate for help. I assisted the women when they birthed their babies, and I watched the old and young die. They taught me about plants that could be gathered from the ground and used to heal. I believe God has created a cure for every ailment." Her shoulders stiffened. "There's much we could be taught, if we would only listen."

"I never really thought about it before," said Ami. "I wonder why more doctors don't try to learn from the Indians if they really do know so much about healing."

Jerusha smiled a wry smile. "Oh, the natives have been treated like dullards and idiots from the first day a white man set foot on American soil. The white man simply cannot understand a different sort of civilized. The white way is the only way. This attitude has caused thousands of men, women and children to die needlessly from hunger and disease. Peace will not truly be found until we can agree with our Declaration of Independence. That all men are created equal. And women," she added, as she swung open the door to her wagon. "You can put the basket over there." She gestured to a bare corner among the piles of boxes and bags.

Ami set the basket down and found a barrel to perch upon. Her father had attended abolitionist meetings, and contributed heavily to the war, though a riding injury from childhood had prevented him from fighting. But problems with Indians seemed like issues dealt with in far-away lands, and most of the people she knew hadn't owned slaves. While she'd considered these atrocities sad and evil, Ami had never thought of them as something she could do anything about, past rolling bandages for the injured from the war and collecting food for the numerous carts that would clatter through, driven by matronly war scavengers. The worst thing that had happened to her during the war years was when she'd been forced to stay shut up in the house for weeks when skirmishes had come too close to the town. Well, and the times there'd been shortages on silk and taffeta. These had been considered miseries almost too great to bear. *What a spoiled, selfish person I was!*

"So much I didn't consider," she murmured.

"Changing the subject, there's a pressing matter I've been pondering. I've been holding off, but the cat's curiosity is eating me alive and with the new folks joining us, more talk is buzzing." Jerusha put a hand on her hip. "Bets have been placed on whether you ran out on your husband or robbed a bank. When folks bring it up to me, I tell them to mind their own business, but I've had more people asking, I suppose because we're friends and all."

Ami's hand flew to her mouth. "How awful! Why would anyone think such terrible things?"

"Young, pretty girl like you, with obvious good breeding and nicer clothes than even the Herschels. You must have been desperate to go away. But like I said, not my matter." Jerusha gave her a slanted look.

"Bernard Regent." Ami covered her eyes. "The man's lips. Like two dead fish, pressed together. And he would've wanted to kiss me eventually, because that's what's expected of married folks. And I just couldn't, Jerusha. I couldn't kiss that man." *And I couldn't give up Mister.*

With this thought, tears ran down her cheeks in trickles, then in torrents.

Jerusha folded her into her earthy embrace and patted her back with gnarled fingers. "There, there," she soothed. "You were asked for more than a body should abide. A woman shouldn't have to marry against her will. It was never the Lord's desire, otherwise he wouldn't have created true love in the first place. Of course, dearie, I was young and impulsive once, too. I ran away from home to marry a man too poor and too idealistic for my very wealthy father. I've never missed the rich things, though I did miss my sisters for a while. I returned home once, to see him on his deathbed. And you know, the old coot probably did himself in by scolding me with his very last breath–this was twenty years later, mind you, with my dear husband cold in the grave." Jerusha chuckled. "I'm sad we couldn't mend the fence, but at least I know I tried."

"Did you ever forgive your father?" Ami asked.

Jerusha squinted through the wagon's little round window and tapped her chin. "Yes, very soon after I ran away. I had too much love in my heart for my husband and the Lord's work to keep room for hate. But I also knew my father was wrong. I'd made the right choice. For a while, I'd have to give it over to God when the anger rose up inside of me. Hatred's a poison, and it's not worth clinging to, not by any rate."

"I hope I can do the same, someday." Ami dabbed at her eyes with her handkerchief. "My father hurt me so badly. I feel like he betrayed everything he was to me."

Jerusha nodded. "It'll eat away at you, and that's for sure. But though you have the right to be angry, you must let go of that right. The anger is warranted, and you needed it at the time to help you get away. But now you must say, 'God, I give my rights to you. Take my anger and give me love instead.' Love is a much greater master. I promise you that."

Ami rested her chin on her folded hands. "You talk like my mama used to."

"Your mama was right," said Jerusha.

Rain spattered the top of Jerusha's wagon. Martha would need help batting down the hatches for the night, but Ami was reluctant to leave the warm, comforting space. As much as she'd come to love Martha's little ones, her wagon was so cramped, noisy and smelly when all of them were forced inside by the rain.

"Thank you . . . for caring so much," she said to Jerusha as she made her way to the wagon's little door.

Jerusha slid her finger beneath Archibald's feet and moved him to his little wooden perch. "Any time you need, child. And I'll be praying for the Lord to give you the peace of mind you desire so you may move on and forgive."

###

On the way back from Jerusha's, Ami encountered Shiloh, who was studying a thick pine on the side of the path. Rain dripped off the brim of his hat, but he paid it no heed.

"Whatcha looking at?" she asked.

He whirled around. "These deep grooves here," he waved to the trunk. "That's from a bear."

"A bear?" she gasped. "How long ago?"

"Maybe a day or two." He leaned closer and sniffed the grooves. "Sap's still fresh."

"Is it a grizzly?"

He sidled up to the markings, measuring with his shoulder. "Nah. Not high enough up the tree, and the markings are too small."

Ami studied the deep ruts created by what must have been powerful claws. She couldn't imagine a beast with larger paws. "Are we in danger?"

Shiloh shook his head. "Not us, but the oxen we lost, especially the one with the sores on his neck, were most likely taken down by one of these fellows. Or a pack of wolves, which I've seen fresh signs of as well. A bear wouldn't go after a buffalo herd, but a few straggling oxen lost in the wilderness? Easy prey."

Ami crossed her arms. "At least it wasn't Indians, probably."

Shiloh shook his head. "Most likely no." He unslung a bag from his shoulder and pulled out a hide-wrapped packet. "I got you something from the Nez Perce people."

"Really?" Ami asked eagerly. Then she sobered. *Should I accept a gift from this man? It seems so forward.*

Shiloh handed her a pair of supple leather moccasins. Brilliant pink and green flowers covered the tops. They were just Ami's size.

"Oh, they're beautiful," she breathed.

"Not something a fine Missouri lady would wear," he said. "But I've seen you stumbling in those clogs you call shoes. They might be thick and protective, but they've got to be pure misery to get around in."

"Everyone else wears shoes like this," Ami said doubtfully. She stared down at her feet.

"Not everyone." Shiloh showed her his own moccasin-clad foot. "I've been wearing these for years. They last an eternity and will make your feet and legs stronger. They take a bit of getting used to, but once your blisters are gone, you'll never go back."

"Thank you," Ami murmured. "It's very generous of you."

"I don't like to see you hurting," Shiloh said. He picked up his bag. "Whelp, I'd better tell the captain about these markings."

14
Fort Kearney

Six weeks on the road. Could it really have been so long? The days were filled with endless, repetitive chores and hard labor. But the evenings were peppered with singing, dancing, and stories. Once Ami had stolen away with Shiloh, Ellie and the Herschel siblings for a moonlit ride across the prairie. She'd never have gone if Shiloh hadn't been along, but she felt completely safe with his broad shoulders ahead of her on the path.

To her immense relief, Captain Reckon had avoided her since the first fireside dance, though he'd shot her mood-filled glares when their paths happened to cross. Ami was used to dealing with men who couldn't get what they wanted from her, so she'd give curt, polite greetings and move on.

The next day, the wagon train approached Fort Kearney. Ami had to admit she was a bit disappointed when it came into view. She'd imagined a grand, stately fortress, almost a castle, complete with gigantic cannons and perhaps a tower or two. Instead, they were met with a building smaller than her father's house, surrounded by walls stained with dust and mud.

Trading posts were clustered around the fort, many fashioned from nothing but canvas and poles. Entire families worked in several of these 'posts.' One member of the family, in most cases a child, would stand outside to call out the best deals for blankets, gunpowder and canned goods. Ami wondered if these were families who had simply given up on the trail and set up shop. Part of her didn't blame them.

While the group set up camp, a few soldiers came out to talk to the immigrants. A young man with a blond moustache, approached Ami while she churned the day's butter supply.

"What's a beautiful young Yankee girl like you doing out on the trail?" he asked, doffing his hat. Ami couldn't help but notice the dull gray beneath the film of dust.

"What's a Johnny Reb soldier doing out in a fort after the war?" she shot back.

His cheeks reddened a bit. "Ma'am, we're here to serve our country. The full United States. Things have been so bad with the Shoshone tribe that the government sent us. They had to find something useful for the prisoners to do." The soldier's smile was quick and hard.

Ami's heart flooded with regret for her hasty words. "My apologies, sir. Thank you for being here to keep us safe."

"Not a problem, ma'am. Not that I have much of a choice. But it's a privilege to watch over a lovely lady like yourself."

Another smile, so boyish that Ami realized the soldier was young, younger than her. Maybe not much older than Ellie. He must have joined up right at the end, even though the Confederates knew the great loss was coming. *And now he's forced to be here, so far away from family. At least I had a choice.*

"Everything all right over here?" Shiloh appeared by her side.

The soldier replaced the hat on his head. "Fine, sir, I was explaining to your lady here how I came to be at this place. She asked, sir. I meant no disrespect." The young man scooted off before Ami could explain she wasn't anyone's 'lady.'

Shiloh stared after the soldier for a moment then turned back to Ami. "You should be careful. Some of these soldiers have been on their own for a long time. They forget how to be civilized."

"He wasn't doing any harm." Ami lifted her chin. "Did you see how young he was?"

Shiloh jabbed at a pebble with the toe of his boot. "I wasn't much older when I joined the Union. If I'd been on the losing side, I'd be right here with him."

Ami swallowed hard. "I forgot you served in the war."

Shiloh shook his head. "Not something I want to remember. What a senseless time. In the first year, I took a bullet to my side. I spent a year in a church they'd set up as a recovery station. When I was strong enough to come back, they put me in as a scout to the outlands. I'd go ahead to find strategic places to camp, keep stock, that sort of thing. I was never forced to take another man's life, though I reckon my scouting was responsible for death of hundreds."

Ami studied him, trying to picture easy-going Shiloh as a hardened war strategist. "There's so much about you I don't know," she murmured, then flushed as she realized she'd said these words out loud.

Shiloh gave a short laugh. "I could say the same for you." He glanced from side to side and then lowered his voice. "I don't even know your real last name."

Ami opened her mouth to tell. After all, it was Shiloh, it could hardly hurt him to know since he was already privy to her secret. But someone moved behind him, and she caught the squinting look of the unkempt woman that never seemed to be far away from her these days. Ami turned away. "Walk with me," she murmured to Shiloh. "Make it look like we're going for water."

He obligingly picked up a bucket as she selected a pail. "Your wish is my command."

Ami glanced behind them as they moved away. The woman made no move to hide her interest, just stared after them, arms crossed over her soiled apron.

Shiloh led the way to one of the several wells that dotted the land in front of Fort Kearney's gates. Ami dropped the large wooden bucket from the lip of the well and waited for the satisfying splash.

Shiloh pulled the bucket up for her. "What's all this about?"

"It's that couple, the Brewsters. Remember how you pointed them out to me?"

"Sure." Shiloh nodded. "I thought at first they might be thieves, but I've changed my mind. They probably are very poor and haven't been around too many fine folks, so they're most likely curious. Plus, let's face it, Miss Tanner. You're quite a lovely lady. You must be used to getting some attention."

He gave her a stare of his own, his eyes twinkling.

Ami shoved his arm a little. "Stop that! Yes, sometimes people do stare for whatever reason. But this is different. I feel almost like . . . they're waiting for something."

Shiloh rubbed his chin. "Waiting for something? Do you plan to sprout wings and fly, Miss Tanner?"

"Kent. My last name is Kent. My first name really is Ami, though. You can . . . call me Ami."

He reached over and ran his finger across her shoulder. Drawing her chin up, he tilted her face gently. "Don't worry, Ami. I told you I'd help watch over you, and I haven't stopped."

"Thank you." Ami lowered her head, just a bit, to hide the look she knew was plastered all over her face. The revelation smacked her right between the eyes. She was smitten with Shiloh, 'completely gone for him' as Francie would say. *But what would we do? Travel with wagon trains our entire lives?*

I could never . . . not after this.

"Ami, it seems like you're already in Oregon and far away from me," Shiloh murmured. "I wish you'd stay here with me and talk for a while."

"I do want to stay with you," said Ami, unable to keep the impatience from creeping into her voice. "But there's so much . . . In the way," she finished lamely. *Oooh. I never have trouble saying what I mean with anyone else! Ever! Why can't I just say it. Spit it out, like Ol' Pat always said. I care for you, Shiloh, but I can't live my life on the trail. I just can't do it.* She balled her hands into fists.

Hurt crept into Shiloh's eyes. "I'm not refined enough for you. Is that it?"

"Of course not. I mean, I wondered at first." She bit her lip. *What a ridiculous thing to say.*

The color drained from his face. "None of us wear our white gloves out here, Miss Tanner." With that, he swung his bucket of water over his shoulder and walked away.

"No. I was wrong. I . . . Oh!" Ami fought the impulse to stomp her foot like a little girl. She grabbed her pail, sloshing half the water out into the dirt, and didn't bother to refill it with the rest of the water in the well bucket.

###

Shiloh stomped back to the circled schooners, his mind foaming over with bitter thoughts. *Shiloh, you fool.* The airy notions he'd allowed to form in his heart, dreams of a home and gentle arms to hold him, scattered like ashes in a storm.

How did I let this come so far? Ami . . . Miss Kent. He'd been so sure of her returned affections. He shook his head. How had he allowed her to use him? All the times he'd gone out of his way to help with her chores. The nights he'd circled her tent to make sure no varmints were bothering her. The ribbing he'd endured from the other wagon teamsters for his errant mooning had been brutal. And they were right. He'd allowed the minx to cast a spell on him, though he'd warned himself from the beginning.

The anger cooled into misery by the time he'd reached the wagon he shared with Joe. His chest burned and his eyes smarted. "Pull yourself together, Shiloh," he muttered. "You're acting like a lovesick schoolboy." He needed a distraction, and there were plenty of tasks to accomplish before bedtime.

Gotta fix that cracked yoke pin. He rooted around the toolbox, searching for a chisel and mallet.

"It'll cost you double." A raspy whisper, hushed but distinguishable, broke through the line of bushes on the outskirts of the circled wagons.

Shiloh froze, mallet in hand. He swiveled towards the sound, straining to hear better.

"Double is too much. We don't even know when we'll see our money." A voice, unmistakably female, whined.

"Elda, be reasonable. You want to see this all go to rot? We'll need a cover, otherwise they'll send someone after us." Another male voice.

Elda? Shiloh's thoughts raced through the names of the wagon train's members. *The middle-aged couple from Marshall's wagon train?* That seemed right.

"Both of you keep it down. If anyone gets wind of this, it's over. Now I want my money in gold."

Shiloh's blood ran cold as he recognized the raspy voice. *What is Reckon negotiating?* He'd scouted for the wagon master twice now and besides the man's womanizing ways, he'd never given any signs of moral corruption. But whatever he planned now couldn't possibly be of good will.

Shiloh scooted closer to the voices, watching for twigs and loose pebbles.

"You'll get your money. Tonight," the second male voice promised.

"I'd better," Reckon said. "Now when are you planning to take action?"

"When the time is right. Be patient," Elda responded.

Feet shuffled through the grass, and Shiloh swiftly crouched behind a wagon wheel and melted into the shadows.

The three plotters never appeared, so he let out a long breath and considered the situation.

Reckon was sore at Ami. *Miss Kent.* That was for certain. But Shiloh found it hard to believe the man capable of causing the girl physical harm. He must have been negotiating for a mule, or an ox. *The man wouldn't hurt anyone.* No matter how jilted he felt.

Though jilting smarts. Agony poured through his mind like molten lead once more, and he leaned his head against the wooden wagon wheel, closing his eyes.

"Shiloh, what in thunderation are you doing under there?" Joe's voice boomed above him.

"Oh. Uh, high time this wheel was inspected," Shiloh stammered.

Joe poked his head under the wooden wagon frame, bushy eyebrows drawn over his bulbous nose. "Didn't seem to me you were inspecting nothin.' Shiloh, it's not like you to take a nap when there's so much to be done."

Shiloh showed Joe the mallet, still clutched in his fingers. "Not sleeping, I promise."

The tightened muscles beneath Joe's heavy beard relaxed. "All right then. Let's get on with the chores. I checked those wheels this morning."

"You should tell me these things so the same task isn't done twice," Shiloh scolded as he crawled out from beneath the wagon. He returned to the pile of tack to find the broken peg, but his heart told him the swirl of feelings that continued to flood through him could not be so easily brushed away.

15
Fallen

Buffalo chips covered the ground like irreverent dinner platters. Ami, Dan, Dave and Ivy collected them in baskets. To be specific, Ami and Ivy gathered them. Dan and Dave played a game of catch, tossing a chip back and forth. The children discovered the dried pieces of manure soared through the air quite well. Some could fly over twenty yards with a well-flicked toss.

"Boys, let's focus on the task at hand," Ami pointed to their half-filled baskets. "We'll need twice as much if we don't wish to come out again before supper."

"Yes, Aunt Ami," the boys chorused, running back to their task with good-natured grins.

Ami picked up the chips quickly, scanning for bugs before dropping them into the basket. *If only Millany could see me now.* She chuckled at the thought of her stepmother's horrified expression. Though she had to admit, when she'd realize what they'd have to use to cook with on this section of the trail she'd probably have been just as appalled. But the flattened patties of manure were plentiful, while wood was scarce. They'd soon learned the fires made with buffalo chips burned hotter and cooked faster, with less smoke to boot.

Out of the entire company, only the Herschel family refused to use the chips. Francie said her father had spent two dollars for a few armloads of wood in the last town. "My mother simply can't abide the idea," she said.

Word spread through camp that Mrs. Herschel rarely left the wagon now. Some people figured she was ill, but Francie told Ami the truth after being sworn to secrecy. "She's been taken by sorrow and fright." Her friend's blue eyes had brimmed over with tears. "She's convinced the Shoshone will scalp us all. Or worse." Francie leaned closer, her brilliant blond hair bouncing along her forehead with every word. "They capture all of us women and take us captive. I've heard horrible things." She shuddered. "Sometimes I listen to the men talk at night when they think I'm asleep. Canvas tents are thin."

Ami studied the bluffs towering over each side of the trail. Though she believed Shiloh when he stated the Shoshone would never attack such a large group of wagons, stragglers were in danger. Indians weren't even the biggest risk here. Bears, mountain lions and snakes covered these hills. He'd relayed this information in a distant, nonchalant manner, a tone he'd taken on since their ill-finished conversation at the well. A dull pang hit her heart, like it did every time she saw Shiloh or thought of him. *Eh, there will be men aplenty in Oregon. Maybe I'll even find Paul.* But it wasn't as easy to slip into this thought as it used to be. Her heart held to Shiloh with tenacious fingers, refusing to let go. Every time she tried to shake these feelings away, she remembered his face as he held that little baby after the fire. *He'd be a wonderful father. I know he would.*

A pile of misshapen brown clumps teetered in her basket. She grabbed the handle and gestured to the children. "Come on, everyone. Time to get back to camp."

A raindrop splashed on the end of her nose. She groaned. She'd fallen so deep into her daydream that she'd completely missed the clouds gathering above them and the unmistakable drop in temperature.

"Blasted rain!" She flew across the ground, prairie grasses snatching at her skirts. "We've had four showers in three days!"

The children scurried after her and they scampered along with several other women and children who'd been gathering chips, trying to shield their baskets from the worst of the rain.

As she neared the wagon, Francie rushed up to her. "Ami, have you seen Maggie?"

"Not today," said Ami, ducking under the canvas awning and pouring her chips into a pile. "Wasn't she going with Ellie and a few others to gather berries?"

Bright red spots stood out on Francie's white cheeks. "Yes, but Captain Reckon called the young people in from their walk ages ago. Remember, the captain said everyone must stay within eyesight of the wagon train since we're in such dangerous territory. I thought Maggie was with her new friend, Becky Masters in their family's wagon." She clasped her hands. "Mother is beside herself. What will we do?" Her voice rose to a wail. "What if she's been captured?"

Dan, Dave and Ivy emptied their baskets and ran off to the wagon, most likely in a race to be the first to deliver the news to their mama.

Ami checked outside. The sudden shower had already burst itself out, the drops turning into drizzle. Francie came out of the tent and stood beside her.

Shiloh, Thaddeus, Mr. Herschel and a few of the other men rode up on their horses. "We're going out to search for Maggie, now, Francie," said Mr. Herschel, a rotund man with a flowing moustache. "Get back to the wagon and tend to your mother."

"But I want to look for Maggie, Father," said Francie. "I'm every bit as good a rider as Thaddeus."

Mr. Herschel scowled. "I don't need to be wastin' time on the search with a girl telling me what she will and won't be doing. You'll do as I say."

Thaddeus gave Francie a crooked smile as the riders turned their steeds and galloped away.

Ami headed to the livestock paddock to check Cavalry.

Francie followed her. "You'll come with me, won't you? You saw Thaddeus. He knows we could help."

"This is a new territory. We have so many more dangers to worry about here," Ami said. "Maybe this time we should listen to your father."

"Pooh." Francie folded her arms. "Did you see them heading off without asking me what I thought? They were going to the river because that's where the group of young people went today. I bet Maggie went back to the bluffs to look for better berries. I know my sister and her sweet tooth."

Ami shielded her eyes and glanced around the camp. Drizzle still fell. People busied themselves, caring for stock and covering fires. They had become accustomed to the rain as a part of life, just like Ami. She could ride in the wet as well as the sun.

"Let me fetch Cavalry," she said.

"Thank you," Francie squeezed her hand. "I'll get my horse too."

In moments, the girls stole out of the camp. Everyone was too busy preparing for the night to notice them leaving.

Driblets still splashed on the leaves above them when they passed under the sparse trees. Ami's sopping bonnet sagged over her eyes. She pushed it back to dangle by its strings.

"We saw the berries over here," Francie called over her shoulder.

The horses moved with delicate steps over the slippery rocks and mud. Ami couldn't help but notice Cavalry's grace compared to Francie's horse, the bumbling Romeo. *Of course, I could have scattered a dozen eggs in Mister's stable and he wouldn't have cracked one of them.* But Mister wasn't there.

Cavalry snorted as though he could read her thoughts.

"The berry bushes are here. See them? Among these rocks." Francie pointed. "I can't believe that girl would come all this way. Father would tan her hide if she were a boy."

Dread pooled in Ami's heart. "But she's not here, Francie."

"Maybe she climbed down the ledge." Francie dismounted, and Ami followed suit. "The berries are pretty thick all down along here. Maggie? Where are you? Yes," her voice floated over the rocks. "There's a ledge here, it's perfectly–aaagh!!!" Her scream was so loud and sudden, Ami nearly jumped out of her skin. She rushed around the ledge to see Francie staring over the side, her eyes wide and her face whiter than the daisies growing along the bluff.

Ami peered over the edge. Far below, at least fifteen feet, Maggie's crimson hat bloomed against the rocks. Her dress was spread out like moss over the stone surface.

"Oh, she's dead, she's dead!" wailed Francie, covering her face with her hands. "What will I do? What will I tell Mother? Why wouldn't she listen?" She sank to the ground. "Oh Maggie!"

"Help me." The voice was faint but unmistakable. Ami poked her head back to check down the bluff. One slender white hand was raised, waving frantically.

Francie peeked between her fingers. "Maggie? You're alive?"

"Yes, but my ankle is hurt," Maggie's voice was choked with pain. "I slipped while I was trying to get to that ledge in the middle, where all the brightest berries are. I landed on this tangle of bushes. I've ever so many scratches, Francie."

"Oooh, Maggie, I'm glad you're not dead. But what are we going to do now?" Francie darted a look at Ami. "How are we going to get her out of there?"

Ami examined the ledges surrounding the crevasse. Maggie was situated in a cradle of rock between the bluffs. The rocks seemed to be about the same height, almost making a 'o' shape around the injured girl. "I don't think we'll be able to get around the bottom so we can climb up to her. Maggie, can you clamber back up the ledge?"

Maggie sat up, pulled her dress free from brambles and tried to rise, but sank back down. "My ankle hurts too much. And it's very slippery. I don't think I can make it."

"What if the Shoshone were coming? Could you climb up then?" Francie's exasperated look was back again.

"No, Francie." Maggie's voice rose in pitch. "I just can't. You'll have to get Papa."

"The men went a different way. They've probably started a war with the Shoshone by now," Ami's shoulders slumped. "It's getting dark. We've got to see if we can get you out of there on our own."

Cavalry nickered and rolled his eyes until the whites were showing.

"I know it's suppertime," Ami went over and patted his neck. "I want to get back every bit as much as you do."

The lasso she kept on the front of her saddle to help round up stock caught her eye. She pulled it off and unrolled it. "Might be long enough." She dangled it over the edge of the cliff.

"What are you going to do with that?" Francie rubbed the tears from her eyes, leaving smudges of mud in their place. "We're not strong enough to pull her up, even together."

"We aren't, but Cavalry might be." Ami lowered the rope to Maggie. "Can you grab that?"

Maggie pulled herself up again, wincing. "No. But I'll try to inch up to the next ledge. I think I could reach it then."

"You can do it, Maggie," said Francie. "Be brave. Think of your nice warm bed and a hot mug of soup once you get up here."

Maggie made a face. "You mean my straw tick in the wagon bed and cabbage marrow broth? Maybe I'll think of my soft feather quilt back in Missouri instead."

Francie tilted her head. "Yes, that might be a better idea."

Maggie pushed up against the rock wall, stopping to breathe every few moments. Her breaths came in short gasps and each movement was agonizingly slow. The clouds hung thick and heavy over the girls' heads, and Ami prayed that God would hold back the deluge until Maggie was safe.

Finally, Maggie made it up to the dangling rope. "All right, I've got it."

"Good girl." Ami breathed a sigh of relief. "Make a loop around your waist. Do you know how to tie a decent knot?"

Maggie gazed up at them, her cheeks covered with small red slashes from the brambles. "I think so. Thaddeus has taught me some."

The rope wiggled and jumped from Maggie's manipulations. Finally she called up, "it's good."

"That's just fine, Maggie," Ami said. "If you slip there'll be something to keep you from falling too far. Hold what you've got for a moment, I'll tell you when to brace."

Ami looped the rope around Cavalry's saddle pommel.

"All right, Francie, you'll need to steady the rope from that side and talk to Maggie while I work with the horse. This will take all our strength combined."

Francie peered over the side and shuddered. "I feel dizzy when I'm close to the edge."

"Imagine how Maggie feels," Ami snapped. "Now let's pray this works."

She pulled Cavalry back until the rope was taut, then braced her feet against a rock. "Here we go. One–two–three. Pull!"

Nothing happened.

"Come on, Francie. There's no one else. We couldn't have done this back home. But we're stronger now. We can do it. Pull!"

The rope slackened, then tightened again.

"I'm moving!" Maggie shouted up. "I'll grab hold of branches and things when I can to lessen the weight."

"Back up, Cavalry. There's a good boy," Ami coaxed.

Cavalry stepped back, and Ami followed. Francie ran her hands down the rope.

In this manner, they continued to pull. Ami's muscles were on fire, and Cavalry's eyes bulged out of his head.

The rope slipped a few inches. Francie yelled and said a few extremely unladylike words she must have learned from the teamsters.

Ami felt as though her arms would be yanked right from their sockets and go tumbling down the side of the mountain like Jack and Jill, but she dug in her heels.

Then came the beautiful moment when Maggie shouted, "I'm here, come get me."

Francie and Ami pulled their way to the edge and grabbed Maggie's arms. They hauled her over the bluff in a heap of calico and petticoats.

Maggie scooted to Francie, sobbing in her lap. "You saved me. Oh, I was so foolish. But you saved me!"

"There, there. We've all done idiotic things in our lives. Remember when I was sweet on the Illish boy?" Francie patted her sister's tangled curls gingerly, leaving smears of blood on the gold.

"Francie, your hands," gasped Maggie. "And yours too, Ami."

Ami checked her palms. The skin was clean gone from both, leaving a bloody mess.

Francie shook her head. "I remember when I'd keep my hands perfectly white. I was so proud of their smoothness." She clicked her tongue. "What a silly thing to be vain about. I could have lost my sister today."

Ami stood on shaky feet and pulled the rope from the saddle. "You'll be getting extra oats tonight," she said to Cavalry.

Francie and Ami helped Maggie onto Cavalry's saddle and led their horses to camp.

The walk back was short, but the sun had become a tiny sliver of orange on the horizon, spilling its eerie glow across the ridges of rock. Ami shivered in the cooling night air. A wolf pack wouldn't hesitate to take down a couple of horses and riders if they were hungry enough. *I must see about purchasing a gun if I'm to remain alone.* Fear crept along Ami's spine. *What will I do in Oregon? How could I ever think I'd just magically find a place to live and be?* Whispered tales flew from the more 'vulgar' women in camp, the women who'd say anything for a scandalized reaction. Stories of soiled doves, of destitute souls who lived in saloons and sold themselves to survive. Or begged in the streets for crusts of bread. Ami lifted her chin. *I am well and of sound body. I will find something respectable to do with my life.*

A long, low howl filled the evening air. *That is, if I return to camp alive.*

When the three girls reached camp, a group of men were gathered on the edge of the wagons. Torches blazed from many hands.

Captain Reckon stalked up and down the line. "We won't leave a single one of them redskins standing!" he was shouting, his face mottled in purple and red. "We'll see how they like stealing our womenfolk!"

"You mean us?" Francie stepped into the torchlight.

A gasp rose up from the crowd. Captain Reckon's jaw dropped. "Er. Yes. How the–" He caught Ami's eye and his face turned scarlet.

"Oh Francie. Maggie!" Mrs. Herschel tottered forward, lurching as though she'd topple to the ground at any time. "Where have you been? I was worried sick! I've been taken by the vapors all day, and your father . . . he's searched everywhere!"

"Except where we could have told him to look," Ami muttered.

After the girls told their story, the men began to snuff out the torches and go about the normal evening tasks.

Martha brought the three girls soup as they gathered around the fire.

Ami's hands felt like they were on fire, but the rest of her felt cold as a January morning. She was thankful for the warmth and the comforting souls surrounding her.

Jerusha hurried over and squatted down beside her. "I came when I heard. Here's salve that could help your hands."

"Tend to Maggie, first." Ami gestured to where the girl lay on a blanket, her foot stuck out before her. "I think she might have broken her ankle."

Jerusha shook her head. "I hope not. Trail life is no place for a broken bone, and we have so much further to go."

Ellie came to inspect Ami's wounds, but Ami waved her over to Francie. "Francie got the worst of the rope burns. I'll be fine to wait."

"Allow me to help." Shiloh brought a steaming bucket and placed it at Ami's feet. He gently took her hands and turned them over. "Whew. Not too bad? I'd say you were a few rope burns shy from losing a finger or two. I have some clean rags here, but this is going to hurt."

"It's fine." Ami spoke through clenched teeth as he set to work. New pain zipped through her skin and up her arm. She fought the desire to slap him away.

"You're full of gumption, aren't you?" Shiloh said. "I'm sorry we didn't listen to you ladies. I was trying to help Mr. Herschel. I should have known you two would go gallavantin ' away on your own." His jaw tightened. "Shouldn't have gone off like that."

"If we hadn't gone alone, Maggie would still be out on that cliffside," Ami said firmly. "And you know it."

Shiloh nodded. "Yes, I do. Good ol' Cavalry. I knew he had it in him."

"I'm very thankful. He stood still as a scarecrow until I needed him to move. It's as though he knew exactly what the stakes were."

"Of course he did," said Shiloh, pouring a little more water over Ami's hands. "God sent an angel to keep him still."

Ami's eyes widened. "You really think so?"

"Sure I do." Shiloh shrugged. "Just like I believe God led the two of you to the very ledge where Maggie fell. And He gave you strength to pull her up when you felt your arms would give out."

Ami bowed her head. "He certainly did. It would have been impossible without Him."

"With faith, all things are possible. Isn't that what Thaddeus said the other day?" Shiloh held her right hand up to the firelight and squinted at it. "I guess that's cleaned."

Ami nodded. "Sometimes it's hard for me to believe God cares about little ol' me and my life, but that's what the Bible says. We're His children and He loves us. I need to remember that every day." She shivered. "I've never been so terrified as when we came back to camp tonight."

"That makes two of us. Captain Reckon told us to stay put for the night, but Thaddeus and I were about to head back out." Shiloh took a bit of salve and rubbed it on her hand. "Look, last time we talked it didn't go very well."

"You mean the time you didn't listen?"

"I mean all the times I haven't listened." His eyes glimmered in the firelight. "I'm listening now, Ami."

Ami sighed. "I don't know what to say."

Jerusha waddled back over to Ami's side. "Did you rub in that salve?" She took Ami's hands and peered down at them. "These look all right." She glanced at Shiloh. "Did you get them plenty clean?"

"I think so, ma'am." Shiloh doffed his hat. "I'll leave you to check my work."

Jerusha examined Ami's hands. "Looks good. I always say cleaning leads to better healing."

"Thank you, Shiloh," Ami gave him a smile.

"Miss Ami. Perhaps we can talk again when you are feeling better?" asked Shiloh.

"I'd like that," said Ami.

In that case, have a good night, Miss Ami." Shiloh nodded to the older woman. "Ms. Jerusha." He walked away.

"How is Maggie?" Ami asked.

Jerusha pursed her lips. "It's a bad sprain, but the bones aren't broken. Still, the pain will be harsh with the jarring of the wagon. 'Course, she's lucky she didn't break her neck. Sometimes brambles are good things in the path of life."

"I'd say," Ami settled back against the wagon with a sigh. *Seems like we've been falling into more of those patches than usual lately.*

16
Taken

Ami adjusted the bucket in her hands and tried not to wince. Two days had passed since the impromptu rescue on the bluffs. Ellie and Martha protested at the amount of work Ami still took on, but she waved them away. They were fortunate to have fresh water for this stretch of the trail, ahead, they'd heard, were the dreaded Alkali pools responsible for poisoning many horses, mules and oxen.

Back home, the slightest headache would have sent Ami to bed for the day; and Brenda might have called for a visit from her father's private physician. Now she'd learned to push the pain to another part of her mind where it sat like a pebble in her shoe, annoying but not debilitating.

Ami dipped the bucket into a pool created by a small spring bubbling up in the middle. The cool water shimmered in such an inviting way that she was tempted to pull off her shoes and dip in her blistered, tired feet. Though Shiloh's moccasins had made a world of difference, they couldn't prevent all aches and pains.

But there was no time. Martha needed the water to boil potatoes for the evening meal, and the task could take over an hour. They were getting down to bare essentials, and Shiloh, Thaddeus, and several other men had gone out on a hunting expedition this evening, Shoshone or not. Bert and Tad had also accompanied the hunting party, promising to share their portion of meat with the Davis family in exchange for the cooking of it.

Two butterflies fluttered by on fragile, paper-thin wings, and Ami paused to watch them. She didn't usually have an entire watering hole to herself. She reveled in the silence, knowing she'd be in the thick of noise and chaos momentarily.

Blue-black designs brushed the air, and the butterflies danced in and out of their own special pattern.

I wonder if they're lovers. Maybe ran away together from all the other butterflies. Ami laughed to herself. But oh, how she envied their freedom. She'd thought running away from under her father's thumb would be freeing, but she'd brought upon herself a new kind of prison. The prison of the never-ending road, the day by day plodding, all the hills and trails mirroring the ones she'd seen the day before that, and the day before that. *What if it's a lie? What if there is no Oregon and we simply survive on the trail until our hearts give out?*

She shook her head. *This type of thinking won't do at all.* Maybe she'd take a short ride on Cavalry before supper to clear her head. The reins would hurt her palms, but everything pained them.

Rough hands grabbed her shoulders, and a filthy cloth was shoved between her lips before she could scream. She gagged and choked as a scratchy burlap bag was yanked over her head. Her arms and legs were bound tightly together before she scarcely had a chance to kick.

"Get her over here, Gus, and be quick about it. Someone could come for water at any moment." The speaker was a woman, with a high, thin voice.

The same evil hands jerked her up, and she was hoisted over something tall. The overpowering scent of dirt and leather filled her nose, and she could only surmise that she'd been draped over a saddle. The beast shifted and balked beneath her.

Then they were moving. A cold terror, stronger than even what she'd felt on the dark ride a few nights before, gripped her throat, and she longed for the ability to scream, even if no one could hear her through the lonely bluffs.

"Gus, we have to camp somewhere soon. The Shoshone are real and no amount of money's gonna pay for our scalps." The grating woman's voice broke through Ami's agony.

They had already halted twice. The first time was, to Ami's vast relief, to allow her to could sit upright on the saddle because her captors feared she might fall off. This was done with much blustering and consternation, because they would not remove the gag or blindfold. Ami's midsection was sore and stretched, as though she'd been churning gallons of butter all day.

The woman had climbed up to ride behind her. Added to Ami's pain was the unpleasant, sour smell of the woman's unwashed body and clothes.

The second stop, they'd yanked out the gag and forced her to swallow a bit of water. This was a blessing, for though the removal of the gag tore skin off her lips, causing them to bleed, her captors didn't replace the cloth and she was able to breathe freely.

Ami was allowed to grasp the saddle horn with her bound hands. This kept her from falling over the side, but knives of pain shot through her arms with every jostle. Greater than this discomfort was the fear of trusting someone with obvious ill intent to guide a horse headed to who knew where.

She'd realized her captors were the couple from the other wagon train who'd been watching her. They must have discovered her identity and decided they could get a ransom from her father. And they were probably right. Even though in his heart and soul her father was probably glad to be rid of her and the problems she'd caused him, he'd still make a big show of wanting her back. He held a prestigious position in their town, and it wouldn't look right to let her go without some attempt to find her.

At least the coolness of evening had settled over Ami's shoulders. The journey would have been unbearable in the heat of the day. She figured they'd most likely be heading back east, but a tiny, silly part of her wished they would take off the horrid burlap bag and she'd find herself in Oregon at last. *I've waited so long to see it, and now I probably never will.*

"Elda, we'll stop up there," Gus's voice barked. "Nice shelter and it'll be hard for anyone to glimpse a fire among those rocks."

"Shoshone don't have to see nothing," Elda said wryly. "They can smell smoke miles off. But I'm guessing that's a good a place as any. Are you sure your brother will be waiting for us near the fort?"

"Sure," came Gus's dry answer. "Left him a message with the storekeeper, didn't I? That storekeeper and I go way back, and my brother knows him too. Can't find a better deal on tobaccy, and he always keeps it special for us."

"One thousand dollars in US gold," Elda cackled. "Daddy must really love you, huh?" she thumped Ami on the back.

"Shouldn't be smacking on her, now," Gus warned. "We don't want to leave a bruise the size of a pinhead. Don't want him taking away any money for damages."

Ami's throat burned with stifled sobs. The pain of being hog-tied to a saddle and taken somewhere against her will was nothing compared to being discussed like a cow at a butcher's auction.

The faces of her friends flickered into her head. Francie, Thaddeus, Martha's children, Jerusha. She'd never even get to say goodbye. And Shiloh, just after he'd been so caring about her hands. *Why couldn't we find time to finally listen to each other?* Tears ran thick and fast beneath the burlap sack.

The mule they were riding came to a sudden halt.

"Here we are. Let's get you down for your beauty rest," said Elda. "Don't think you need this anymore."

The burlap sack was roughly pulled from Ami's head. Fresh breezes caressed the chapped skin of her face and she gulped in the cool air like spring water.

"Get on down." Elda pointed to the ground. "You should see yourself, you look like a fish. Fancy lady indeed."

Ami glared at her. *They aren't going to hurt me, they're too intent on getting money. I'm not giving them the satisfaction of discussion.*

Ami sat on the rock Elda indicated.

Gus pulled out sticks of wood from his pack and began to build a fire, while Elda mostly barked out orders and fussed with their saddlebags.

Ami did some math in her head. Three people with two mules. They would be back to Fort Kearney in three days or less if all went well. And then what? Would Gus's brother have a schooner outfitted for them? Would they keep her hogtied in the bed of a wagon until they reached Memphis, or send word to her father to meet them somewhere along the trail?

She studied the faces of her captors. Gus had flat, sunburnt cheeks, with a slack jaw and a vacant stare. But Elda was shrewish.

Her beady eyes seemed to catch everything. *She has a plan, or she'd never have attempted this.*

As if reading her thoughts, Elda nodded. "Sure is sure, you gave us quite a fit getting you alone. That scout of yours was always watching you, wasn't he? Thank goodness his stomach got the better of him and he decided to go huntin,' or we might never have whisked you away."

"He's in for a surprise now." Gus gave a rotten-toothed grin. "His girly's going back to papa."

Elda folded her arms. "Seems we're doing you a favor. Why anyone would leave three square meals and silk notions for life on the trail beats me all hollow. You want to tell me why you left, Missy?"

Ami blinked, realizing this was the first question that had actually been addressed to her. She pressed her lips together in a tight line.

"Gonna be uppity with me, huh?" Elda drew her hand back. "I'll smack that insolence right out of you, Girl."

Gus caught her hand. "No, you won't, Elda. Remember, damaged goods."

The fire was stoked, and Elda boiled dried meat and beans from a tin to make a sort of soup.

Gus untied Ami's hands so she could eat. "Don't think about running away," he hissed. "The hills are full of Shoshone and they'll take you off in a heartbeat."

Ami gazed out into the endless bluffs. They were in enough danger as it was. She'd only seen two weapons in her captors' possessions. A rifle that Ed kept by his side and a long blade slung in a sheath across Elda's hip.

Ami ate slowly and savored each bite, though the food was flavorless and dull. Even if she had the strength to mount a horse at this point, she wouldn't know which way to go. She wondered if the wagon train would attempt to find her. The Herschel girls had beloved parents to care for them, but she had no true family at camp. Though her friendships were real, they were surface, and she could hardly expect anyone to brave the dangers of the prairie to search for one girl.

Far off across the plains, a cougar screamed. Gus perked up from where he sat by Elda across the fire. "Too close for comfort,' he muttered.

Ami's heart hammered against her ribs. The idea of a trip back to Memphis seemed torturous, like picking out the stitches to an exquisite embroidery. Tears dripped down her cheeks again, and she turned away so her captors wouldn't see.

Finally, she fell into a fitful sleep, her head pillowed against the wall of the bluff.

17
Chances

Shiloh fastened a deer carcass to the rack he'd rigged up from boards and ropes and stepped back. The hunt had been successful, and good thing, since few settlements awaited them for the next several days. The other men from the hunting party laughed and joked as they skinned prey and cleaned weapons. Everyone was in a better mood since they'd found fresh meat for roasting on spits and stew pots. They'd need to keep a vigilant guard tonight. Wolves and other predators would be sorely tempted by the tantalizing scents in the wind.

On the way to the springs to clean up, Shiloh encountered Martha Davis. The woman studied the ground as she walked, muttering to herself. She'd have run plumb into Shiloh if he hadn't reached out to stop her.

"Mrs. Davis, is everything all right?" he asked.

"Mr. Talon, thank goodness!" Martha acted like she wanted to hug him, but she stopped short when she saw his messy hands. "I'm beside myself with worry, and I don't know who to turn to."

"What can I do for you?" Shiloh's heart stilled in his chest. His instincts, which rarely served him wrong, told him that something terrible had come about. "Is . . . Ami . . . Miss Tanner, all right?"

Martha caught his gaze and looked away. "She's been gone for hours. Went to the springs and never returned."

"Thunderation." The word slipped out and Shiloh didn't bother to apologize. "No one's gone to search for her?"

Martha wrung her hands. "That's just it. Captain Reckon told me she's run off. He said she decided to go with the Brewster couple, that Gus and Elda. You see, they turned back. To Missouri. They didn't even take their wagon; I don't know how they'll make it back. Why would Ami up and leave without even saying goodbye? My children are beside themselves." A tear dribbled down her cheek. "Why would she take such a dreadful risk?" Her voice cracked, and the next words came as whispered. "Why didn't she say goodbye?"

Shiloh clenched his fists as everything snapped together in his mind. Elda and Gus constantly watching Ami. The hushed conversation he'd overheard between the Brewsters and Captain Reckon. *Blasted bounty hunters.*

He stomped over to the paddock. Cavalry grazed peacefully with the rest of the stock. This confirmed his suspicions. *She'd never leave her horse.*

Anger danced before his eyes in white, hot spots. He stomped towards the captain's wagon.

Reckon was shaving himself, using a tiny round mirror.

Shiloh grabbed the man and jerked him up so fast Reckon almost slit his own throat with the razor.

Reckon sputtered, spitting flecks of shaving cream from his mouth. "What are you thinking, Boy?"

Shiloh shoved him up against the wagon. "You know why I'm here, and you know why I'm angry. You'd better answer me this question or I'll let the whole camp know how greedy and underhanded you are."

Reckon gave him a crafty smile. "Are you referring to Miss Tanner? She told me how homesick she was. Cried on my shoulder and gave me a goodbye kiss, too. I sent her off with two capable chaperones and my blessing. Sorry if she didn't think you were good enough for a farewell, Boy."

Shiloh's grip tightened. "You and I both know that's a lie. She wouldn't have left her horse, and she would've told Mrs. Davis her plans."

Reckon's eyes bulged out, but he still shrugged. "The girl gave me her horse. She chose to ride one of the Brewster's mules. I guess she wanted to tell me how she'd appreciated my care and consideration over the trail."

Shiloh squeezed harder. *It'd be so easy to crush the life right out of this man.* His breaths came quick and hard.

The captain's cheeks darkened, and he gasped, 'You'll hang for this, Boy."

Slowly, Shiloh relaxed his grip and let the man fall against the schooner box.

The teamster slumped to the ground, choking and gasping.

"Be glad I answer to a higher power than myself," Shiloh growled. "You're not worth breaking a commandment for."

With that he stalked away.

###

The next morning dawned on Ami's exposed face, since Elda and Gus had no tent and they all lay, like brittle leaves, on the bare ground.

A slight breeze wafted through the air and the new sun peeked out, fierce and ready to show its mettle. Shade was scarce as the small group set out once more.

Gus and Elda picked out a path that gave a wide berth to the wagon trail. Ami marveled at the audacity of her captors. *We're three people in the middle of the open plain. Yes, we'd see a Shoshone a mile away, but where would we run? We'd be fish in a barrel, ready to be shot.*

In the hazy meanderings of her mind, she wondered how it would feel to be run through by an arrow. At this point it seemed preferable to captivity.

Several times, she was told to walk beside the mules to save their strength. The animals were packed to their capacity of food and supplies, including several skins of water. Gus and Elda were stingy with the water, since most of the water sources would lead them to close to the wagon trail and might lead to an unwanted encounter. *But the mules must drink before too long, and then what?*

Ami studied Elda's face. *How much of this journey was fueled by shrewdness and how much by greed?* Their lives could depend on this answer.

Gus's eyes roved over the hills and flats in a constant search. He'd jump when pheasants and prairie chickens flew up before him and swore once when a dragonfly landed on his shoulder. *He's afraid*, Ami realized with a start. She began to pray harder, under her breath, because she hadn't uttered a word since her capture.

When they stopped for a break, Gus folded his arms and stared out across the plains. "I don't like this one bit, Elda. I've said it before, and I'll say it again. A thousand dollars is no good to anyone if they're scalped."

Elda stirred their campfire with a stick. "Too risky to return to the wagon tracks. Captain Marshall will hear we've gone. He might put two and two together, and then what? He's bound to think we headed back to the fort."

Gus poked at Ami. "Hey, Girl, anyone know who you are? Anyone thinkin' you'd be running back to Daddy?"

Ami shook her head but refused to speak.

Elda grabbed Ami's wrist, and a jolt of pain ran up her arm. "Look here, Missy. Not going to do any of us a good turn if you don't talk. We need the information now. Do you want us to die out here? You'll be first, and we'll leave your bones to be picked clean by the buzzards." She leaned closer, her lips drawn back into a snarl that reminded Ami of dead coyotes they'd seen by the side of the road.

Ami took a swallow of water. "No, no one knows who I am." The lie burned her lips, but she knew her best chance was to return to the wagon tracks. *Maybe I can escape and follow the tracks back.*

Gus chuckled, a dry laugh that sounded like the wheeze of a mule. "You don't lie well, do you? It would serve you better to learn how." He jerked his head to Elda. "Don't you worry none. Reckon said he'd cover our tracks."

Reckon? Captain Reckon's behind this? Ami gasped. How could he be so cruel? Surely he'd been thwarted by a pretty lady before. *But maybe this isn't the first time he's exacted revenge.* If he was evil enough to work with Elda and Gus, anything was possible.

Gus continued. "We'll find the wagon trail and stay close, but only follow them when there's good visibility to see if someone is coming after us."

Edna grunted a rare agreement. "That's the best way."

A wild hope sprang up in Ami's heart. If they were close to the trail, maybe she could get away from her captors and follow the tracks back to Martha's train. *But if I do, won't they just catch me again? If Captain Reckon did this, he could tell them anything. He could make up something bad about me. What if I'm caught by the Shoshone instead?* Horrible as life back home would be, it seemed preferable to living as an Indian captive. She'd heard the stories of women forced to be slaves.

After they ate, Gus gave the mules a few swallows of precious water. He wiped sweat from his brow. "We'll have to get back to the tracks anyway, Elda. Mules gotta drink and we haven't found a waterin' hole all day."

After what Ami considered far too short of a rest, they moved back out into the blazing sun. Hour after hour the mules waded through the ankle-deep dust.

Despite the grim situation, a deep swell of relief flooded through Ami at the ability to travel so much faster than the maddening wagon's pace. Even though her brain told her they were going the wrong way. Away from freedom. Back to a life of unwanted domestication.

By evening, the stretch of wagon ruts flowed before them.

Gus dismounted and studied the road. "Probably not a camp within earshot. We should reach the fort in two days or fewer. And most importantly," he tilted his head. "There's a river flowing nearby."

The mules pawed the ground and tossed their heads.

When they reached the tiny spring, Elda grudgingly untied Ami's hands and allowed her to wash her face and undo the bandages.

Ami expected to see dark, angry welts beneath the bandages, but to her amazement they seemed much better, and the pain had lessened. She studied her hands. Just two days ago, they'd seemed like her biggest frustration. But since her abduction she'd hardly noticed them. *Jerusha's salve must truly work miracles.*

While the mules slurped the water with greedy grunts, Gus and Elda began to argue again.

"That girl eats too much," Elda snapped as she prepared the paltry dried beef and bean soup she made every day. "Needs to start earning her keep."

"Elda, don't be foolish," Gus pulled the mules back from the water and drove their lead stakes into the ground. "She'll earn plenty when we get paid our thousand dollars."

"Still." Elda pursed her lips and glowered at Ami. "I'm not gonna be no ladies' maid to her either." She yanked Ami to her feet and pointed to the trailside. "You can gather buffalo chips. Might have to go a ways. Anything we could burn has been picked clean by the last train."

Gus glowered at Elda. "Don't you think she'll run off?"

Elda glared at him. "Sure she will, Gus. Straight down a wolf's throat." She snapped back to Ami. "You're smarter n' all that, ain't you girl? Or maybe not so much smart as scared of your own shadow."

Ami stumbled down the rugged trailside. At first a sort of giddiness filled her, a disbelief that they would let her go on her own. But as she stopped to pick up the few buffalo chips she could find, a lone wolf howl filled the air. Darkness would cover the world in moments, and she had no fire, no weapon and no way to survive the night. The pure evil of Elda's mind astounded her. *She knew fear would consume me. I'm her slave, and there's nothing I can do about it.*

It took a long time to fill her apron halfway, and she dared not stay longer. *This will have to do.* Gus had warned Elda not to strike her, but Edna didn't hold to being ordered around. If Ami displeased her, she'd get revenge in some way. *A slap is better than death by wolves.*

The campfire glowed brighter as she neared it. Her hands ached. Perhaps since Ami didn't run away, Elda would have mercy and not tie them again. Her head buzzed with strategies. This close to the tracks, she could surely find a way to escape and catch up with the train. But travel at night was impossible, and she was exhausted. She would try again tomorrow. She lifted her chin. After all, she was a Kent, and Kents didn't give up.

A rock skittered through the grasses to her left side. Digging her nails into her palms, she peered through the now velvety darkness. "Who's there?" she called.

No answer.

Probably a raccoon or bobcat. She shook her head and pushed forward to the light and the people with weapons.

18
Night Settles

As Ami gnawed on a chunk of stale bread the next morning, the rumbling of wagon wheels announced a train was passing their sparse campsite.

"We gotta try to buy some supplies," said Gus. "We don't have enough good food for another day, and we're at least that far from Fort Kearny. The mules need oats, Elda, and I'll die out on the desert ground if I have to eat another bowl of this gruel you've been making."

Elda put her hand on her hip and pushed back a strand of greasy hair that had fallen before her eyes. "Gus, if you're going to be an all-fired whiny baby about your vittles then you go on and get something. I'll just stay here with Missy and make sure she minds her manners."

Gus took off his hat and fanned himself. "All right then. I'll go see if I can rustle up something."

"You'd better not spend more than a quarter, Gus. We don't have nothing to spare 'til we get our reward money."

"A quarter's fine, Elda." Gus shuffled off in the direction of the wagon tracks.

Elda glanced over at Ami's hands. "I'm not gonna tie you up again now, since we might get a visitor from the train. Doesn't look like they're stopping for this water hole, but we might have some stragglers." She tapped her chin. "We'll be telling them you're our daughter who's addled in the head. And if you say anything to the contrary, it'll go badly for you." She rubbed her hands together. "Gus is worried about your papa, sure, but anything could go wrong on the trail. And your father's not going to believe a word you say after you lit out and ran away from him."

Ami's shoulders stiffened. Thankfully, Gus and Elda hadn't thought to search her person and the small pouch of gold coins she always carried still hung heavily around her neck, buried beneath her undergarments. Could she pay the Brewsters for her freedom? Fifty dollars was a far cry from a thousand. They'd be more likely to steal it and take her back anyway. After all, Elda was right about her father. She would never regain his trust after she'd run away. He might even have her locked up in an asylum of some sort. *Millany would love that.*

But the wagon train . . . if she waited until tonight, maybe she could follow the migrants. If she could take a mule, it wouldn't take long to catch up. Perhaps a kindly family would accept a gold piece in exchange for riding with them to her group.

Yes, Elda and Gus would follow when they discovered her missing. But what else could she do? Maybe the family would hide her for more gold.

I'm putting a lot of hope in a kindly family that might not even be real, Ami thought wryly. But she had to try.

Elda sat across from her with the waning fire between them, watching her with shrewish eyes, the musket slung over her lap. The heat of the day approached with haste, and flies buzzed around the unwashed dishes from breakfast.

Elda passed the time by telling stories of her and Gus's exploits, which were alarming and fiendish. They'd been working as wagon train bounty hunters for years. "Many the young child we brought back, or the cheatin' wife," Elda patted her musket in a satisfied manner. "But yours is the biggest purse we've earned." She gave a contented sigh. "Good enough for me, I says. Maybe we can settle down in Nebraska and leave the trail life for always. Or maybe we'll build a ferry. Let the customers come to us and such like. Do my heart good not to have to hear the beggin' and hollerin' for once."

She continued with talk of this nature, droning on and on.

Ami closed her eyes and tried to block out the awful stories. She thought of Shiloh. His sweet smile. The way he'd comforted her when she'd given up Mister. The feeling of his arms around her when they danced that night at the fire.

No sense torturing myself. She opened her eyes to blissful silence.

Elda's head slumped forward, her chin touching her chest. To Ami's astonishment, a light snore came from her open mouth. *She's asleep! The trail must have caught up with her at last.* She studied the musket. Elda's grimy hands were wrapped around it in a death grip. *Can't try to take it, she'll wake up for sure.*

Ami rose as swiftly and silently as possible, taking quick stock of the camp. Gus had taken a mule, but the other one, Rosa, was placidly eating the sparse grass beside the pool. She was no Cavalry, but better than nothing.

Ami's breath came in short gasps as she checked Rosa's bridle and tack. Elda could lift her head and stare at her with those beady eyes at any moment. Or Gus would meander over the hill, and all would be lost.

The safety of travelling during the day was worth the risk. She'd have to skirt around the wagon train and then let the immagrants find her on the trail. Maybe come up with some story about getting separated from another group. The mule could carry her with the train. With a single rider, Rosa could go for days without dropping.

She cinched up the saddle. The saddlebags of supplies were piled beside Elda, but there was no time to load anything. She'd have to rely on the goodness of strangers. Otherwise, she'd just starve until she reached her group.

At the last minute, she grabbed a full skin of water and hooked it on the saddle. Climbing on Rosa, she tapped the mule's sides. "Get going, girl," she whispered in the long, swiveling ear.

Fortunately for their journey, the plain flattened into a mesa and Rosa didn't have much trouble picking her path. On the other hand, cover was hard to come by.

Ami passed as close to the wagon tracks as she dared, hoping to goodness not to encounter Gus on his return. The train, which must have consisted of over a hundred schooners, was slowing already. As she continued, her plan developed. She'd pass them this evening. Elda and Gus would search through the train the first thing in the morning, if she was lucky. She'd need to hole up somewhere, hidden to the side. If she made it until the morning, she'd travel beside the train for a day or two until Elda and Gus had given up. *Oh!* She sighed. It was the worst plan in creation. *I'll be captured within an hour.* But she had to try. "God, with you all things are possible," she prayed. "Please help me get away."

In a short time she'd passed the train. The terrain became rockier. Worried Rosa might step wrong and break a leg, she was forced to move closer to the trail. Every rock that bounced across the ground made her heart jump in her throat.

Finally she had to stop. Rosa's coat was slick with sweat and her giant, gentle eyes rolled back with every step.

A stream bubbled ahead of them, and Ami dismounted and led Rosa to the edge. "All right, girl. You can have a sip. But we can't stay here."

She refilled the water skin and stood on the rocky edge of the pool, staring into the bluffs. She hadn't forgotten the Shoshone, but at this point she was more afraid of seeing white folks.

A low growl rumbled through the rocks. Ami's hair stood on end and fear clutched her by the throat with cold fingers. She didn't have a gun, or a knife, or fire. Nothing but a stout stick that was too raw to burn.

She turned slowly, the staff clutched in her hands.

The tiny eyes of a black bear squinted back at her. She'd never seen such a beast so close, and its sheer enormity, its wildness, struck her senses.

"I know you're hungry," Ami said shakily. "But you leave me alone, hear? Don't come near me."

The bear sniffed the air with such nonchalance as only an animal with no predators could have. It inched closer and gave a snarl.

Maybe if I just stand still. Maybe it already had dinner.

The bear lunged at her with surprising swiftness considering its clumsy build. Snapping jaws reached for her throat, and death filled the beady eyes.

Ami swung her stick with all her might, hitting the bear square on its nose.

The bear jumped back and pawed at its face.

Rosa plunged and snorted, foam forming on her nostrils. Thankfully, Ami had tied the lead well or the mule would have run off into the wilderness.

Ami darted back a few steps, trying to put Rosa's body between her and the bear.

The bear turned its focus on Rosa, and the mule lashed out with her front hooves. Ami closed her eyes.

The crack of a revolver rang out through the rocks, once, then again. The bear froze for an instant, backed away, and lumbered off into the rocks.

Ami sagged onto the ground. Her riding habit stuck to her skin, and sweat poured down her face. She wanted to curl up into a ball and sob with relief, but . . . who owned the revolver? That person could be a worse threat than even the bear. She gripped her stick tightly and rose to her feet. *I'll die before I go with Gus and Elda again, and we'll see what kind of reward they get.* "Who's there?"

"Ami." The voice was quiet.

She swung her stick out towards the sound. "I'm not coming back with you, Gus. You'll have to kill me first!" Her voice rose to a high, terrified note, despite her brave words.

A man grabbed the stick before it hit his face. "Hey, Ami. It's me."

"Shiloh? What on earth?" She stood still, allowing this realization to take hold in her mind, then all at once her energy evaporated and she slumped into his arms, boiling tears running down her cheeks.

Shadow bounded up between then, covering her hands with doggy kisses.

"Oh, you came. How did you find me?" Her words unraveled in a stammer. "I didn't . . . think . . . you would come."

Shiloh caught her up to his chest and stroked her snarled, matted hair. "Of course I came. I've been watching over you since last night, actually. Those two old bats kept pretty fierce guard and I didn't want to have to resort to violence unless absolutely needed."

Ami leaned back and studied his face, the face she'd thought she'd never see again. "I remember, I heard a crashing in the bushes. I thought it was a raccoon. Was that you? Why didn't you tell me?"

Shiloh laughed and stroked her cheek. "I couldn't count on this beautiful face to keep a secret. I didn't want us to have to run away in the dark. I was waiting until the right moment to whisk you away, figured we could join up with the train nearby."

"Oh, but we can't," Ami's shoulders sagged. "Because this group is going to be searching for us. Elda and Gus will surely have spun a story about losing me. They're so evil and tricky."

Shiloh rubbed his beard. "Yes. If only you'd tarried a bit longer. You just had to go and get away by yourself, couldn't wait for a hero to rescue you." He gave her a wink.

Ami put a hand on her hip. "And how could I have possibly known you were coming to my rescue, Mr. Talon?"

Shiloh put a finger to her lips. "Shh. Those folks you ran away from could be coming up this trail any moment. We have to get going." He glanced around then raised an eyebrow. "I know one way to keep you quiet. If you'll allow me."

He dipped down quickly, his lips meeting hers before she knew what was happening. She almost pulled away from sheer surprise but the longing within her won out, and she returned the kiss, ignoring the smart from her still-chapped skin. Wrapping her bandaged hand around his neck, she pulled him closer.

Though it seemed an eternity until he drew back, the kiss still didn't seem long enough. Her eyelashes fluttered against her burning cheeks. "I–suppose that was a good way. Though I can do what I'm told . . . Shiloh."

Shiloh brushed her hair back from her face and gave her the tender smile she'd missed so much. "Don't always. Your sauciness makes you beautiful, you know that? Now let's get going."

He went back into the bushes and led out his horse. "You want to ride Griego or do you prefer the mule?"

"Rosa and I get along just fine." Ami patted the mule's velvety nose before mounting. As she eased into the saddle, a thought struck her. Her throat went dry. "Shiloh, what if we get arrested for stealing the mule?"

Shiloh's sigh floated on the air between them. "Ami, the Brewsters tried to steal *you*. You're a grown woman. They had no right to try to collect a bounty."

"Depends on who you talk to," said Ami. "Get my father to find a doctor who'll say I'm addled in the head, and they might just prove it."

"Don't you worry." Shiloh clicked his tongue to the horse as they reached an easier passage. "I'd keep the mule as payment for your suffering. The old fools. But if it'll ease your conscience, we'll leave the mule with Marshall's wagon train once we trade her for Cavalry. If Elda and Gus ever catch up, they can pick her up there."

The reality of what he was saying sank in. "You mean, we can't travel with our train the rest of the way?" Before he could reply, the pieces began to fall together. *Of course. If I stay with my train, the Brewsters will follow us and try to capture me again. Maybe even bring their brother and his friends. They could follow me all the way to Oregon.* Tears slipped down her cheeks, and she rubbed them away so they wouldn't blur her vision. *I'll never be free. Father will always figure out how to find me.*

Shiloh turned and studied her with kind eyes. "I think you know we can't."

"We?" Her question hung in the air, like a hovering dragonfly, looking for a place to light.

After a long silence, Shiloh replied, "I've been thinking about this on the way here. Reckon's in on this. He might act like nothing's wrong when we get back. After all, he already got his money. But if the Brewsters show up looking for you, there's no telling what he'll do."

"Can we even fetch Cavalry?" Ami gasped. "And say goodbye?"

Shiloh dipped his head. "I think so. Reckon's not gonna want to admit he sold you up the river. You aren't the only one who's used the trail to escape from somebody. Doesn't bode well for a trail captain to get mixed up with bounty hunters." He rubbed the back of his neck.

"Nope, we'll waltz in like nothing happened. Hopefully he'll pretend along and let us go on our way. If not, we'll have a talk with Marshall and expose him for who he is."

"I think we should expose him anyway," Ami said hotly. "Serve him right for being so evil." Then another glaring thought struck her. "Shiloh, where on earth will we go after we fetch my horse?"

"Give me a little time to think it over," he said. "Do you trust me to figure something out?"

"Of course I do," she said softly.

Shiloh pulled back on the reins and stood in his stirrups, searching the hills surrounding them. "I'd say we're a day's hard ride from our wagon train, but one other group is between us and them. Smell the smoke in the air?" He squinted.

"Met up with an old friend of mine at Fort Kearney. He said he was scoutin' for the train coming right behind us. In fact," He gave her a grin, "I would have joined up with him if it weren't for a beautiful girl I'd have to leave behind. Let's see if we can get some vittles from him."

"But what if Gus and Elda catch up with us?" Panic crept into Ami's voice.

"Then it would be our word against theirs. But I wouldn't worry too much. Old Ezekiel won't give us away if we explain the situation."

19
Ezekiel

Shiloh and Ami worked to keep their mounts in stride during the journey; Griego was eager to strive forward to camp and civilization and kept breaking into a canter, while Rosa was content to dawdle at a slow trot, almost a walk. This would have been a frustration at any time, but with the possibility of Gus and Elda popping up from behind a bluff, it was even more maddening.

Shadow ran circles around them until Shiloh scolded him. "You're going to get your head stomped on, you silly dog." He pulled Shadow up in front of him on the saddle, where the dog balanced like a bird on a fence, his tongue lolling out.

"The Brewsters only have one mule," Ami reminded herself. Gus was no small weight, and their beast couldn't have carried the two of them for very long, if they attempted to ride double at all. *Unless they bought a horse from the wagon train.*

A friendly air hung about the circle of schooners as they approached. Two women hung laundry on a make-shift line strung between two of the wagon frames. They rushed up to meet Ami as she dismounted.

The elder of the two pushed back her sunbonnet and gave Ami a concerned smile. "Hello, there, dear. Why are only the two of you riding out here by yourself? Surely it can't be safe with all the Shoshone in these parts."

"No, it's not," Ami agreed.

Shiloh came up and put his arm around Ami's waist. "My wife and I are just passing through. We've had some hard times we'd rather not speak of right now."

The younger woman's eyes filled with pity. "Don't we all. The trail's been harder than any of us could imagine. Three of our people have been lost since Missouri, and one man had his foot crushed a wheel today." She dabbed at a tear with the corner of her apron. "The good Lord have mercy on us."

"He's a good Lord indeed," said Shiloh. "Say, do either of you two ladies know where we can find ol' Zeke?"

"He's four wagons down around the way." The older woman pointed. "Got a black cloth hanging over the front. You can't miss it."

"Thank you so much." Shiloh tugged on his horse's lead. "Nice to meet you ladies."

"I can't believe you lied about us being married," Ami murmured as they picked their way through the camp, invoking several stares from the company.

"Hopefully it won't be a lie for long." Shiloh tilted his head back and gave her a grin.

Ami couldn't help but smile back, and a glowing heat flowed through her body, all the way to her toes. *He wants to marry me. Oh, he really does love me. Of course he does, or why would he have come for me?*

They approached the wagon with blackened canvas nailed to the front. A man with an impossibly wiry frame, wearing a faded striped shirt, fried griddlecakes over an open flame. He caught sight of them and leapt to his feet, his long white beard flapping in the wind.

"Shiloh Talon, as I live and breathe!" He grabbed Shiloh's hand and pumped it up and down. "Good to see you. I heard you were a few trains ahead, but you wouldn't catch me trying to find you in this territory! What in the world are you doing here? Hope you didn't risk your neck just to see me."

"No, no." Shiloh removed his hat and held it to the side. "Ezekiel, this is Ami Kent."

Ezekiel took her hand, furrows travelling down his brow. "You're the one I heard about," he said in a low tone. "You're worth a king's ransom."

Stark realization hit Ami in full force. *If the Brewsters hadn't kidnapped me, it would only have been a matter of time before someone else had recognized me.* She bowed her head. *I'd never have made it to Oregon. There's no getting around it. I'll have to hide out somewhere else.* A feeling of hopelessness enveloped her, until she caught Shiloh's eye. She stood straighter. *I'm not by myself. I'm with him. Somehow, we're going to make it.*

"Don't look much like the photograph while you're wearing that getup," Ezekiel waved a hand at Ami's clothes.

"Still caught the eye of a couple of bounty hunters," said Shiloh grimly. "She got away, but they'll be on our tail. We'd like to ask for your help, Ezekiel."

"Of course, of course." Ezekiel glanced around. "What can I do for you?"

"Do you have any trail vittles or extra water skins to spare? We're gonna have to run ahead of these folks and it might mean travelling through more dark stretches than I'd ever dare."

"I can pay." Ami reached for the pouch of precious gold coins hanging from her neck.

Ezekiel stretched out his hand. "No need for that. I have a few old skins you can take and welcome. We shot a few deer yesterday, so there's plenty of fresh meat and I stocked up good at the fort." He gestured to their mounts. "Why don't you tie them somewhere, I'll rummage around and see if I can find something you can use for a saddlebag."

He disappeared into his wagon. Muted cursing and banging drifted out from behind the black blanket.

"Shouldn't we hurry?" Ami whispered to Shiloh. "This is nice of him, but Elda and Gus could be here any moment."

"Don't you worry about that," Shiloh whispered back. "If Zeke is on our side, he'll take care of them when they come through. Their mule is liable to get loose, spooked or both. And no one on this wagon train will object. Ol' Zeke is somewhat of a legend. If he does something, they'll back him up, no questions asked."

Ezekiel emerged from the wagon, two bulging saddlebags. "This ought to do until you get back to your outfit," he said.

They loaded the bags on the mule and horse. Griego gave a reproachful whinny.

"I know, I know, fella." Shiloh patted his nose. "We have some hard riding to do, and you want your rest and good oats. All in time."

Shadow barked and bounded around Shiloh's heels.

"At least one of us is ready for adventure," said Ami.

She pulled a coin from her purse and held it out to Ezekiel. "Please accept this."

"Oh no." Ezekiel folded his arms. "So many folks have given to me freely of what they had. It's the only reason I've lived long enough to grow this beard. T'would be a sin to accept payment. No, young lady, if you want to make an old man happy then take the opportunity to help other folks when you can. It's the only payment that matters."

Back on the wagon tracks. Ami and Shiloh had nothing but the pale moon to keep them company.

Barn owls swooped overhead, their bright faces catching the moonlight and scaring Ami half to death at every appearance. She and Shiloh dared not to speak above a whisper, which meant neither one of them could hear to have a conversation over the clattering of hooves.

Shiloh finally drew up his horse and raised his hand.

Ami urged Rosa forward so she could hear him speak.

"We've gone all we can tonight," he said hoarsely. "Rosa could go longer, but I've already pushed Griego enough. We must stop and camp somewhere. We'll have to build a fire and take turns watching it, otherwise the wolves will be after the horses." He sighed. "Which makes us more visible to the Shoshone. It's a risk we'll have to take."

Ami nodded. Stopping was dangerous. Travelling at night was dangerous. She watched Shiloh as he dismounted and crept along the side of the track, searching for a good stopping place. *He put himself in so much danger coming back for me. Maybe it would have been better to go along with Gus and Elda. At least I wouldn't be risking both of our lives.*

Shiloh glanced up at her, his face illuminated by moonlight. "There's a bit of a hollow here. No water, but the animals already had a good draught at the camp, and they can have a bit from ours.

Ezekiel gave us plenty and there are a few good places up ahead. We can reach them tomorrow."

They unpacked their sparse supplies. Shiloh had a blanket. He cleared a section of ground from rocks and sticks and rolled it out. "You can sleep there," he gestured to the pallet. "I'll keep watch after I build a fire."

"You need sleep too," Ami protested.

"Listen." He took her hand gently. "You've been through more frights in the last few days than most people deal with in a lifetime. Fear takes a toll on your soul. You need rest."

Ami removed the bandages from her hands for the last time and threw them into the bushes. After taking off her shoes, she pulled the blanket over her. She shivered. The night air was always a bit chilly, but tonight seemed colder than ever.

Shiloh busied himself getting a small fire together. He pulled out Johnnycake and dried strips of meat and handed them to Ami. "As much as I'd like to roast a piece of that venison Zeke gave us, the scent would bring every animal across the country running. I'd rather not take the chance." He tossed a few chunks of raw meat to Shadow, who gulped them down and begged for more.

"This isn't proper." Ami blurted out. "I mean, what will we do? Even with the necessity of you rescuing me folks are never going to understand. I might as well sew a scarlet letter to my shirtwaist. Please don't think me ungrateful," she added lamely. "And I really don't know what else we could have done. I could be eaten by a bear right now, and that's much worse than being looked upon as disgraceful."

Shiloh chewed his bite of dried meat, his brow furrowed. "I would never allow you to be eaten by a bear. But why worry so much about what other folks think? God has seen everything we've done. We haven't done anything wrong, besides lie about being married, and I believe He'll forgive us for that."

Ami stared into the fire's embers. "I suppose it's different for a man. Sometimes people let that sort of thing slide, like with Captain Reckon. But in my hometown . . . no one would ever speak to me again. Scandal is a disease no one wants to catch."

Shiloh reached over and touched her arm. "Ami, isn't that part of the reason why you left? To get away from prying eyes and judgmental hearts?"

Ami snuggled down into the blankets. "I suppose the string of scandalous acts I've committed in the last two months would already send me over the edge as far as ever being respectable again. I'm a good Christian woman, though, and spending the night alone with a man, no matter what the reason, is over the top."

Shiloh frowned. "I see what you're saying. Though I hope you aren't afraid of me, Ami. I would never take advantage of you like that."

"Oh, Shiloh." She clasped her hands. "I could never be afraid of you."

He took her hands between his. "You're so cold." He rubbed her fingers and blew on them. "Let's get you a little closer to the fire. I'll watch for sparks." Pulling her mat closer, he smiled. "There, that's better."

"Thank you," Ami murmured. "I'll always be grateful to you."

"Could you have more feelings than just gratitude for me, dear Ami?" Shiloh's voice was wavering, almost pleading.

"Yes," Ami almost whispered.

"I love you, Ami," Shiloh replied. "I meant what I said today at the wagon train, it wasn't a jest. I don't want you to feel compelled because of our situation, but . . . would you consider marrying me?"

A long silence filled the night, pinpricked only by the mournful song of the crickets.

Wild, beautiful hope sprung up in Ami's heart. The eternity of Shiloh's arms around her, his calm voice to soothe her spirits always, through harsh and beautiful times. The steadfast courage and fierce dedication he held for those he loved.

But she sighed, and everything settled back down, like dust on the trail after the schooners had passed. "I can't live on the trail, Shiloh. It's not the life for me. I'm not looking for anything fancy, but I'd like to settle down in a home. With children. Could you handle that kind of change?"

Shiloh's eyes glowed in the firelight. "I see myself with you, Amethyst Kent. Any other sort of life doesn't seem worth living. I made that decision when I came after you. This is forever. I'm not married to the trail. It's a living, but I'll find another way."

Ami swallowed. "Do you mean that?"

"With all my heart." Shiloh put another log on the fire. Sparks danced up to the sky in a whirling dance, and Ami's heart danced with them.

20
Back to the Schooners

Ami awoke stiff and damp from the morning dew. She gazed at the scrubby prairie bushes thinly shielding them from the path.

Shiloh covered the waning coals of the fire with a thick layer of sand. He gave her a grin. "Good morning, Beautiful."

A trembling hand went up to pat her hair. Ami had no mirror or body of water to check her reflection, but 'beautiful' was the last word she'd use to describe herself this morning. *What I wouldn't give for a bath and a change of clothes.* She grimaced. *I'd be thrilled with a hairbrush.*

She settled for washing her face and arms with a bit of their precious water and running her fingers through her snarled hair before she rolled it into the knot she'd had it in for most of the trip's duration.

"Were you up all night?" she asked Shiloh.

He rubbed his eyes and nodded. "How could I sleep when I could stare at your face instead? Don't worry about me. I'm used to going for days without slumber. During the war, sometimes it meant the difference between life and death."

Ami rose and picked up the bedroll to shake it out. "When you think about it, we've been in a sort of war ourselves."

"With all the bounty hunters and bears, I'd say so." Shiloh lifted the saddle over Griego's back and cinched it up. "I'll rest when we reach the wagon train. Shouldn't take us long to get there."

As they finished loading the horse and mule, Ami gazed back at the track. "Wonder why the Brewsters haven't caught up with us?"

Shiloh chuckled. "I can tell you why. Ol' Zeke led 'em on a wild goose chase. The man would give away his last crust of bread but he can lie like a dog." Shadow gave him a reproachful stare until Shiloh scratched his floppy ears.

Ami's stiffness in the saddle was beginning to work itself out faster than before. She marveled at how quickly she'd become used to this life. Sleeping on the bare ground, completely exposed to the mercy of the elements. *Thank goodness we haven't had rain since I was taken.*

They continued to follow the trail. The going was easy in the cool of the morning, before the sun rose with its fiery wrath. Birds began to peep from various perches and far off, they heard a stream trickling over rocks.

Shiloh put a hand to his ear. "There's the water. The animals can drink soon."

"I've been thinking about . . . when we reach the wagon train," said Ami.

Shiloh turned in his saddle and smiled. "You think we can ask Thaddeus to marry us? I hope he'll say yes."

Heat crept over Ami's face, the way it did every time she thought about them getting married. "Yes, Shiloh, that would be wonderful. But I've been thinking about Oregon. If we find another group to journey with and make it to the end, my father has probably already alerted authorities throughout the state. Even if we get married . . ."

"You mean, *when* we get married," Shiloh put in.

"Yes, of course. *When* we get married. I'm always going to be afraid. I'm always going to worry that another bounty hunter will come along. A thousand dollars is a lot of money, and evil people like Gus and Elda aren't going to care if we're married."

Shiloh's hands tightened on his reigns. "I'll protect you, Ami."

"I know you will." Ami dipped her head. "But you can't watch me every moment. I don't want to forever be looking over my shoulder and waiting for my past to catch up with me."

"Have you ever thought that maybe . . . your father believes you were taken against your will?" Shiloh said softly.

Ami swallowed hard. "Yes." A pang went straight to her heart as she admitted it out loud. "And many times, I've begun a letter to explain myself." She grimaced. "I wish I'd been able to forgive him enough to tell him. I was so hurt and angry." A tear trickled down her cheek. "I should have. Maybe this wouldn't have happened."

Shiloh turned in the saddle, his eyes soft. "But it might not have changed anything. And if you sent a letter he would know your path and might have sent for you sooner."

Ami pursed her lips. "It's true. I've thought it over so many times, Shiloh. What would God have me to do?"

Shiloh frowned and rubbed his jaw. "I won't begin to try to speak for God. It's a conundrum, that's for sure. In the meantime, I'll talk to some people when we get back to the train. We can't trust Captain Reckon as far as we can throw him, but some of the teamsters working with him are good folks. The man who shares a wagon with me is trustworthy. He might have an idea of where we can go."

"All right. I think we should both pray about it as well." Ami tried unsuccessfully to keep the schoolmarm tone out of her voice.

A grin broke over Shiloh's face. "You're the very best. Of course we will."

That night, long past dusk, campfire lights winked at them from across the plains. None too soon, for they had almost run out of water.

Relief flooded through Ami's soul at the thought of seeing the people she'd come to love and care for so dearly. But then her heart immediately sank. *We'll have to leave them shortly. Can I bear it?*

In front of her, Shiloh sat up straighter and squared his shoulders as though the same thought process was going through his head.

They approached the paddock on the outskirts of the train. Joe stood guard, scanning the prairie with a glassy stare.

He turned and started. "Shiloh Talon, ain't you a sight for sore eyes!" He clapped him on the back. "And Miss Tanner, we thought you'd gone and left us for greener lands." He gave Shiloh a wink. "Guess she decided she had something worth coming back for."

"Guess she did," said Shiloh. "Hey, Joe, don't tell anyone we're back until we talk to the captains, you hear?"

Joe sobered. "Sure can do, Shiloh, but you ought to know. Captain Reckon high-tailed it outta here yesterday morning with no explanation. Took his wagon and a few other teamsters with him. Captain Marshall's in charge now."

Shiloh's face lit up. "Old coot's conscience must've caught up with him. Or maybe those Brewsters paid him more than I'd thought."

Ronald squinted at Shiloh. "Come again?"

Shiloh laughed. "Isn't important right now. I'll go have a talk with Captain Marshall."

Captain Marshall's face darkened beneath his thick moustache as Shiloh explained his story. "Always something that didn't sit right with me about them Brewsters. If they catch up with us, they can have their animal, but they aren't welcome to be a part of this group. If I'd known they were bounty hunters I'd have thrown them out at Fort Kearney. Two things I hate in this world." He spat at the ground. "Rattlesnakes and bounty hunters. And if given the option, I believe I'd choose the snakes." He tipped his hat to Ami. "You're a woman of your own mind, free to go where you will. Your secret is safe with me. I'm glad you got back in one piece."

"I'm glad as well," Ami replied, though she felt nothing she'd uttered had been so understated. She longed to be free of the formalities and find a place to bathe and dress her hair. Not in the manner of the trail, but like she used to. *To feel like my old self. For only a brief time.*

Shiloh and Ami walked back until they'd almost reached Martha's wagon, trying to ignore the stares and whispers surrounding them.

Shiloh tugged on Ami's hand by the wagon's edge. Low conversation and giggles from Martha's children filled the air.

"I have some things to tend to, my love," he whispered into her ear. "I'll part with you now and see you in the dawn's early light."

Somehow the poetic words fit the moment, even though unusual for plain-spoken Shiloh. "My heart will follow you," Ami replied.

Mayhem broke loose when she entered the firelight of Martha's camp. The children clung to her sodden, muddy clothing and Ellie burst into tears. Martha gave her a hug so tight Ami thought she'd squeeze the life out of her.

"You have to tell us everything, everything that happened to you," said Ivy, her blue eyes shining.

"Aw, I bet it wasn't that much," little Dave scoffed.

"Wait until I tell you about the bear," said Ami.

The children's mouths fell open.

"Merciful Heavens!" exclaimed Martha.

"But not until I get a decent wash," said Ami.

21
Following the Sunrise

Two weeks later, Ami walked down the wagon path towards the man she loved. His face was lit up by the golds and reds of the sunrise and a happiness she'd never seen in any person.

Flower chains had been woven and strung along the sides of the trail by Ellie, Francie and Ivy, while Maggie, still recovering from her ankle, had barked out orders.

The girls all wore their very best dresses, the ones their mothers had forbid them to remove from trunks by pain of death. But Mrs. Davis and Mrs. Herschel also donned their finest clothing. Many of the men wore vests, or at least clean shirts.

The change in clothes and the happy atmosphere had a magical effect on the immigrants. They all stood straighter, seemed lighter. The months of hard toil and trials seemed to melt off their shoulders.

Jerusha arranged a cloudy veil, on loan from a woman who'd been married right before she'd begun the journey to Oregon, around Ami's shoulders. "We should have a wedding every week," she whispered. "Does everyone a world of good."

As light as Ami's heart felt, she wished with all her might her mama could be with her. And even . . . *Father.* She shook away the sadness and continued to move towards her beloved.

Ami paraded past rows of people who had become dear to her, but there was only one face she could focus on, and that was Shiloh's. He stood up straight, his sober mouth betrayed by shining eyes brimmed with tears.

Since that day, a lifetime ago, when Ami had decided to run away to Oregon, she'd never felt so certain about anything in her life.

Though she moved on weary feet, her heart bounded before her, urging her on.

Shiloh held out his hand and she accepted it. He squeezed her fingers and pulled her hand to his chest, where his heart thudded against it.

Thaddeus put down the fiddle he'd been playing and picked up his Bible. He flipped to the middle and looked up, surveying the crowd. "Dearly beloved, we are gathered here today . . ."

Thaddeus came to the vows. "Do you, Miss Amethyst Tanner, take Shiloh Talon to be your lawfully wedded husband?" He said this loudly, then whispered, "Amethyst Kent?"

Ami gave Shiloh a sideways glance. *He must've told him at the last minute so we could be really, truly married.*

Ami uttered the two sacred words, wondering if any woman of the age, since Eve had been drawn from Adam's rib, could have spoken them with such love as filled her heart.

The ceremony was short. No party awaited them, no banquet or sweetmeats. Thaddeus didn't even have time to pull out his fiddle again for a dance. The sun was rising, and they'd lose the day's few cool moments if they delayed any longer.

Friends pressed small gifts into Ami's hands. Tiny cakes, handkerchiefs, and other items she knew were precious and they could ill afford to lose.

Jerusha pulled her down to give her a kiss on the cheek. "Knew you'd do all right, Darlin." She handed Ami a tiny silver box. "Here's some of my salve to keep with you." She pursed her lips when Ami raised her eyebrows. "Don't look so surprised. I knew you'd be leaving the moment you came back. Godspeed to you both."

Everyone immediately changed back into their trail clothes and within an hour, the wagons were ready to continue their monotonous journey.

As Ami passed Martha's wagon, Shiloh grabbed her hand and pulled her into the shadows. "Hello, Mrs. Talon." He kissed her soundly.

She giggled. "Hello, Mr. Talon."

His face radiated with joy, but slowly, a dark shadow crept over his handsome features. "I promised you I would figure out a way for you to be safe, and I believe I have, but I'm not sure what you'll think of it."

She took his hand and kissed it. "I trust you."

Shiloh pulled her close and spoke softly. "It's been two weeks with no sign of the Brewsters. Ol' Zeke must have been able to throw Gus and Elda off our path. At any rate, Captain Reckon left their little cart at the camp when they kidnapped you. Since they took their mules there was no way to transport it anyhow. We must not have noticed it since it was probably at the camp where Zeke was and lost among the other schooners. Anyway, if they found it, they probably picked it up, which would've slowed them down even more. I don't think we'll need to worry about the Brewsters."

"But there will be others . . ." The same lump filled Ami's throat that always did when she thought about being kidnapped again. But now she had Shiloh . . . her husband. Tingles went down her spine. *So much more to lose.*

"A small group of wagons will branch off for the state of Montana at dawn tomorrow," said Shiloh. "We've been seeing more alkali pools, and Captain Marshall believes the wagon train is too big to feed and water the herds properly at one time. We can go with them, but we'll only have our horses and an extra mule to carry supplies. I've sold my half of the wagon to Joe. It'll be weeks with only a tent for shelter and food scavenged from the wilderness and any towns we cross. From what I understand, they are few. I know very little about Montana, I've never been there." He cupped her chin in his gentle hands. "But I've heard it's beautiful."

Tears filled Ami's eyes. "I will miss the people on this train, but I will go where you go, my Love."

They were interrupted by Dan and Dave, who bounded up and clutched Ami's skirts. "Aunt Ami, Aunt Ami, Ma says your leavin' again."

"Yes." Ami gazed down at the smudged faces, choking on her words. "I will always remember you boys. You be good for your mother. You'll be in Oregon with your daddy before you know it."

She picked up the small valise she'd used to pack the few belongings, mostly practical, she'd allowed herself to keep. Any fancy things remaining would go to Ellie and Martha.

Shiloh squinted at the sun. "Looks like we'll be moving any time. The wagons are set to branch off tomorrow, so we have one more day to spend with our friends."

"Then I'll savor every moment," said Ami.

Ami awakened in the shadowed confines of a wagon.

The rumpled blanket beside her was empty. Shiloh must have gone to get everything together and let her rest a bit longer.

Shiloh and his partner had cleaned out their shared wagon yesterday as a surprise. This would be the only time they'd have shelter, besides a flimsy canvas tent, until they reached Montana. Who knew what would happen after that?

Mrs. Talon. Married. She giggled and hugged herself beneath the blankets. What a ridiculous notion, and so beautiful, and so serious, all at the same time. Only once had she been gripped by a panic at what she'd done. It was so forever. So permanent. But one glance of Shiloh's eye and all peace was restored. He was a good man. *The best man for me. He travelled two days back on the beast-infested trail to find me. I'd bet Paul Amos would never have done that. And Bernard Regent wouldn't have taken one step on the path for fear of muddying his shoes.*

She quickly dressed and brushed out her hair, then pinned it up, taking just a bit more care than normal.

The dawn air was cool and refreshing. Martha was busying herself by the fire as usual. She looked up quickly and smiled. "Good morning, Ami."

Ami gave her a hug. "Good morning. I can't believe I'm leaving you today. I'm sorry I won't be able to accompany your family all the way to Oregon."

"It's better than knowing you've been dragged back to Memphis," Martha said in a low voice. "And Ellie's been stronger on the trail. Jerusha gave her some sort of brew that's made such a difference in the girl, I barely know her. But of course we'll miss you." She pulled a crumpled paper from her apron pocket. "Here's the name of the town we'll be living in. Please do write and let us know you're safe."

"Of course I will." Ami tucked the paper away. "Oh Martha, if it wasn't for you, I never would have come! I'd be married to a horrible man and I'd never have met Shiloh at all! Or any of these other wonderful people."

"God works in mysterious ways." Martha glanced up, a tear shining on the end of her nose. "Go safely, my friend."

Ellie arrived, lugging a pail of water. She set it down and gave Ami a fierce hug. "Goodbye. I shall miss you so."

Francie and Maggie came to join in on the goodbyes, and Thaddeus stood off to the side.

Ami shook his hand. "I hope to hear of you becoming the best preacher man ever," she said.

Thaddeus nodded solemnly. "By God's grace, it will happen."

Shiloh came behind her and took her hand. "My love, it's time. The wagons are lining up for Montana."

Jerusha waddled up. "Thank the Lord. I'm not too late." She gestured to Ami's friends surrounding them. "Let us pray for these good people and send them off on their way."

Everyone bowed their heads, and Jerusha gave a sweet prayer of guidance and protection. The words, though simple, were profound, and Ami felt as though God was right there in the midst of them.

How God has protected me! she marveled. *Through countless dangers, past bears and wolves and hostile people. He has led me through to love. And He will lead me to a new home in Montana, so long as I follow His voice.*

ANGELA CASTILLO

Epilogue

Wind whistled around the walls of the snug cabin, somewhere in Montana's Beartooth mountains. Ami stroked Shiloh's tousled hair, and he smiled in his sleep.

Shadow raised his head and gave a soft whine until she reached down to scratch behind his ears. He gave a contented sigh and settled back down at his place at the foot of the bed.

Ami crept over to the small shelf where a lantern cast its glow in a precious halo against the wall. Once the light was gone, they'd be enveloped in belligerent, unending darkness, until the weak winter sun shone through the windowpanes and Shiloh headed off with thel; faithful Shadow to check his traps.

The trail to Montana had taken two more agonizing months, but they'd had each other. Her gold coins and money Shiloh had saved from his scouting had been enough to purchase building supplies and home essentials. Quarrels sprang up but were quickly doused with prayer and love. Through it all, Ami never regretted her choice. Though her heart did hold one sorrow.

The flame flickered and teased, as though it were saying, "It's time. It's time."

Ami rushed to a box on the mantelpiece and rummaged through it until she came upon them; a pen and ink, an envelope, and a precious piece of paper. She'd purchased these items on the first day, in the first town, before they'd started on the trail.

She opened the ink and dunked her pen inside.

"God, give me the courage and the strength," she prayed.

Then she began.

Dear Father,
All is well.

The End

About the Author

Angela has been writing stories since she created her first book with a green crayon at the age of eight. She's lived all over Central Texas, but mostly hovered in and around the small town of Bastrop Texas, which she loves with unnatural fierceness and features in many of her books. Angela has four wild children, a husband who studies astrophysics for fun, and a cat.
To find out more about her writing and learn how to receive a FREE short story, go to http://angelacastillowrites.weebly.com

Excerpt From

The River Girl's Song

Texas Women of Spirit
Book 1, Available on Amazon in
paperback, Kindle and audio.

http://www.amazon.com/The-River-Girls-Song-Spirit-
ebook/dp/B00X32KBL0/ref=pd_rhf_gw_p_img_1?ie=U
TF8&refRID=18DCQ0M4FSR2VYKTRJ15

1

Scarlet Sunset

"We need to sharpen these knives again." Zillia examined her potato in the light from the window. Peeling took so long with a dull blade, and Mama had been extra fond of mash this month.

Mama poured cream up to the churn's fill line and slid the top over the dasher. "Yes, so many things to do! And we'll be even busier in a few weeks." She began to churn the butter, her arms stretched out to avoid her swollen belly. "Don't fret. Everything will settle into place."

"Tell that to Jeb when he comes in, hollering for his dinner," muttered Zillia. The potato turned into tiny bits beneath her knife.

"Don't be disrespectful." Though Mama spoke sharply, her mouth quirked up into a smile. She leaned over to examine Zillia's work. "Watch your fingers."

"Sorry, I wasn't paying attention." Zillia scooped the potato bits into the kettle and pulled another one out of the bag. Her long, slender fingers already bore several scars reaped by impatience.

"Ooh, someone's kicking pretty hard today." Mama rubbed her stomach.

Zillia looked away. When Papa was alive, she would have given anything for a little brother or sister. In the good times, the farm had prospered and she chose new shoes from a catalogue every year. Ice was delivered in the summer and firewood came in two loads at the beginning of winter. Back then, Mama could have hired a maid to help out when the little one came.

She and Mama spent most of their time working together, and they discussed everything. But she didn't dare talk about those days. Mama always cried.

"I might need you to finish this." Mama stopped for a moment and wiped her face with her muslin apron. "I'm feeling a little dizzy."

"Why don't you sit down and I'll make you some tea?" Zillia put down her knife and went to wash her hands in the basin.

Water, streaked with red, gushed from beneath Mama's petticoats. She gasped, stepped back and stared at the growing puddle on the floor. "Oh dear. I'm guessing it's time."

"Are you sure? Dr. Madison said you had weeks to go." Zillia had helped with plenty of births on the farm, but only for animals. From what she'd gathered, human babies brought far more fuss and trouble. She shook the water off her hands and went to her mother's side.

Mama sagged against Zillia's shoulder, almost throwing her off balance. She moaned and trembled. The wide eyes staring into Zillia's did not seem like they could belong to the prim, calm woman who wore a lace collar at all times, even while milking the goats.

Zillia steadied herself with one hand on the kitchen table. "We need to get you to a comfortable place. Does it hurt terribly?"

Mama's face relaxed and she stood a little straighter. "Sixteen years have passed since I went through this with you, but I remember." She wiped her eyes. "We have a while to go, don't be frightened. Just go tell your stepfather to fetch the doctor."

Zillia frowned, the way she always did when anyone referred to the man her mother married as her stepfather. Jeb had not been her choice, and was no kin to her. "Let me help you into bed first."

They moved in slow, shaky steps through the kitchen and into Mama's bedroom. Zillia hoped Mama couldn't feel her frenzied heartbeat. *I have no right to be afraid; it's not me who has to bring an entire baby into this world.*

Red stains crept up the calico hem of Mama's skirts as they dragged on the floor.

A sourness rose in the back of Zillia's throat. *This can't be right.* "Is it supposed to be such a mess?"

"Oh yes." Mama gave a weak chuckle. "And much more to come. Wait until you meet the new little one. It's always worth the trouble."

Mama grasped her arm when they reached the large bed, covered in a cheery blue and white quilt. "Before you go, help me get this dress off. Please?"

Zillia's hands shook so much she could hardly unfasten the buttons. It seemed like hours before she was able to get all forty undone, from Mama's lower back to the nape of her neck. She peeled the dress off the quivering shoulders, undoing the stays and laces until only the thin lace slip was left.

Another spasm ran through Mama's body. She hunched over and took several deep breaths. After a moment, she collected herself and stumbled out of the pile of clothing.

When Zillia gathered the dress to the side, she found a larger pool of blood under the cloth. Thin streams ran across the wood to meet the sunlight waning through the window panes. "There's so much blood, Mama, how can we make it stop?"

"Nothing can stop a baby coming. We just have to do the best we can and pray God will see us through." "I know, Mama, but can't you see... I don't know what to do." Zillia rubbed her temples and stepped back.

Mama's mouth was drawn and she stared past Zillia, like she wasn't there.

Mama won't want the bed ruined. Zillia pulled the quilt off the feather tick and set it aside. A stack of cloths were stored beneath the wash basin in preparation for this day. She spread them out over the mattress and helped her mother roll onto the bed.

Thin blue veins stood out on Mama's forehead. She squeezed her eyes shut. "Go out and find Jeb, like I told you. Then get some water boiling and come back in here as fast as you can."

Zillia grabbed her sunbonnet and headed out the door. "God, please, please let him be close. And please make him listen to me," she said aloud, like she usually prayed.

Parts of her doubted the Almighty God cared to read her thoughts, so she'd speak prayers when no one else could hear. At times she worried some busybody would find out and be scandalized by her lack of faith, but unless they could read thoughts, how would they know?

None of the urgency and fear enclosed in the house had seeped into the outside world. Serene pine trees, like teeth on a broken comb, lined the bluff leading to the Colorado River. Before her, stalks littered the freshly harvested cornfield, stretching into the distance. Chickens scattered as she rushed across the sunbaked earth, and goats bounded to the fence, sharp eyes watching for treats.

"Let Jeb be close!" she prayed again, clutching her sunbonnet strings in both fists. She hurried to the barn. Her mother's husband had spent the last few days repairing the goat fence, since the little rascals always found ways to escape. But he'd wanted to check over the back field today.

Sounds of iron striking wood came from inside. She released the breath she'd been holding and stepped into the gloomy barn.

Jeb's back was towards her, his shirt soaked through. Late summer afternoon. A terrible time for chores in Texas, and the worst time to be swollen with child, Mama said.

"Jeb, Mama says it's time. Please go get the doctor."

"Wha-at?" Jeb snarled. He always snarled when her mother wasn't around. He swung the axe hard into a log so it bit deep and stuck. The man turned and wiped the sweat from his thin, red face. Brown snakes of hair hung down to his shoulders in unkempt strands. "I got a whole day of work left and here it is, almost sunset. I don't have time to ride into town for that woman's fits and vapors. She ain't due yet."

Zillia fought for a reply. She couldn't go for the doctor herself; she'd never leave Mama alone.

Jeb reached for the axe.

"There's blood all over the floor. She says it's time, so it's time." Zillia tried to speak with authority, like Mama when she wanted to get a point across. "You need to go Jeb. Get going now."

When it came to farm work, Jeb moved like molasses. But the slap came so fast Zillia had no time to duck or defend herself. She fell to the ground and held her face. Skin burned under her fingers. "Please, Jeb, please go for help!" she pleaded. Though he'd threatened her before, he'd never struck her.

"Shut up!" Jeb growled. "I'll go where and when I wish. No girl's gonna tell me what to do." He moved away, and she heard the horse nicker as he entered the stable.

Wooden walls swirled around Zillia's head. The anger and fear that coursed through her system overcame the pain and she pushed herself up and stood just in time to see Jeb riding down the road in the direction of the farm belonging to their closest neighbors, the Eckhart family.

They can get here faster than the doctor. First common sense thing the man's done all day. "Please God," she prayed again. "Please let Grandma Louise and Soonie be home."

Blood, scarlet like the garnets on Mama's first wedding ring, seemed to cover everything. The wooden floor slats. Linen sheets, brought in a trunk when their family came from Virginia. Zillia's fingers, all white and stained with the same sticky blood, holding Mama's as though they belonged to one hand.

The stench filled the room, sending invisible alarms to her brain. Throughout the birth, they had played in her head. *This can't be right. This can't be right.*\

The little mite had given them quite a tug of war, every bit as difficult as the goats when they twinned. Finally he'd come, covered in slippery blood that also gushed around him.

Over in a cradle given to them by a woman from church, the baby waved tiny fists in the air. His lips opened and his entire face became his mouth, in a mighty scream for one so small. Zillia had cleared his mouth and nose to make sure he could breathe, wrapped him in a blanket, and gone back to her mother's side.

Mama's breaths came in ragged gasps. Her eyelids where closed but her eyes moved under the lids, as though she had the fever. Zillia pressed her mother's hand up to her own forehead, mindless of the smear of red it would leave behind.

The burned sun shrank behind the line of trees. No fire or lantern had been lit to stave off the darkness, but Zillia was too weary to care. Her spirits sank as her grasp on Mama's hand tightened.

At some point Mama's screams had turned into little moans and sobs, and mutterings Zillia couldn't understand. How long had it been since they'd spoken? The only clock in the house was on the kitchen mantle, but by the light Zillia figured an hour or more had passed since Jeb left. When the bloody tide had ebbed at last, Zillia wasn't sure if the danger was over, or if her mother simply didn't have more to bleed.

A knock came at the door. The sound she had waited and prayed for, what seemed like all her life. "Please come in." The words came in hoarse sections, as though she had to remind herself how to speak.

The door squeaked open and cool evening air blew through the room, a blessed tinge of relief from the stifling heat.

"Zillia, are you in here?" A tall, tan girl stepped into the room, carrying a lantern. Her golden-brown eyes darted from the mess, to the bed, to the baby in the cradle. "Oh, Zillia, Jeb met Grandma and me in town and told us to come. I thought Mrs. Bowen had weeks to go, yet." She set the light on the bedside table and rushed over to check the baby, her moccasins padding on the wooden floor.

"No doctor, Soonie?" Zillia croaked.

"Doctor Madison was delivering a baby across the river, and something's holding up the ferry. We passed Jeb at the dock, that's when he told us what was going on. The horses couldn't move any faster. I thought Grandma was going to unhitch the mare and ride bareback to get here."

In spite of the situation, Zillia's face cracked into a smile at the thought of tiny, stout Grandma Louise galloping in from town.

An old woman stepped in behind Soonie. Though Grandma Louise wasn't related to Zillia by blood, close friends called her 'grandma' anyway. She set down a bundle of blankets. A wrinkled hand went to her mouth while she surveyed the room, but when she caught Zillia's eye she gave a capable smile. "I gathered everything I could find from around the house and pulled the pot from the fire so we could get this little one cleaned up." She bustled over to the bedside. "Zillia, why don't you go in the kitchen and fill a washtub with warm water?"

Though Zillia heard the words, she didn't move. She might never stir again. For eternity she would stay in this place, willing her mother to keep breathing.

"Come on, girl." Grandma Louise tugged her arm, then stopped when she saw the pile of stained sheets. Her faded blue eyes watered.

Zillia blinked. "Mama, we have help." *Maybe everything will be all right.*

Grandma Louise had attended births for years before a doctor had come to Bastrop. She tried to pull Zillia's hand away from her mother's, but her fingers stuck.

Mama's eyes fluttered. "Zillia, my sweet girl. Where is my baby? Is he all right?"

Soonie gathered the tiny bundle in her arms and brought him over. "He's a pretty one, Mrs. Bowen. Ten fingers and toes, and looks healthy."

A smile tugged at one corner of Mama's pale lips. "He is pink and plump. Couldn't wish for more."

Grandma Louise came and touched Mama's forehead. "We're here now, Marjorie."

Mama's chest rose, and her exhaled breath rattled in her throat. Her eyes never left Zillia's face. "You'll do fine. Just fine. Don't—" She gasped once more, and her eyes closed.

Zillia had to lean forward to catch the words.

"Don't tell Jeb about the trunk."

"Mama?" Zillia grabbed the hand once more, but the strength had already left her mother's fingers. She tugged at her mother's arm, but it dropped back, limp on the quilt.

A tear trickled down Grandma Louise's wrinkled cheek. "Go on to the kitchen, Zillia. The baby should be nearer to the fire with this night air comin' on. Soonie and I will clean up in here."

"I don't want to leave her," Zillia protested. But one glance at her mother's face and the world seemed to collapse around her, like the woodpile when she didn't stack it right.

How could Mama slip away? A few hours ago they'd been laughing while the hens chased a grasshopper through the yard. They'd never spent a night apart and now Mama had left for another world all together. She pulled her hand back and stood to her feet. She blinked, wondering what had caused her to make such a motion.

Soonie held the baby out. His eyes, squinted shut from crying, opened for a moment and she caught a hint of blue. Blue like Mama's.

Zillia took him in her arms. Her half-brother was heavier then he looked, and so warm. She tucked the cloth more tightly around him while he squirmed to get free. "I have to give him a bath." Red fingerprints dotted the blanket. "I need to wash my hands."

"Of course you do. Let's go see if the water is heated and we'll get you both cleaned up." Tears brimmed in Soonie's eyes and her lip trembled, but she picked the bundle of cloths that Grandma Louise had gathered and led the way into the kitchen, her smooth, black braid swinging to her waist as she walked.

Zillia cradled the baby in one arm, and her other hand strayed to her tangled mess of hair that had started the day as a tidy bun with ringlets in the front. What would Mama say? She stopped short while Soonie checked the water and searched for a washtub. *Mama will never say anything. Ever again.*

The baby began to wail again, louder this time, and her gulping sobs fell down to meet his.

Zillia sank to the floor, where she and the baby cried together until the bath had been prepared.

As Soonie wrapped the clean baby in a fresh blanket, Jeb burst into the house. He leaned against the door. "The doctor's on his way." His eyes widened when he saw the baby. "That's it, then? Boy or girl?"

"Boy." Soonie rose to her feet. "Jeb, where have you been? I saw you send someone else across on the ferry."

Jeb licked his lips and stared down at the floor. "Well, ah, I got word to the doctor. I felt a little thirsty, thought I'd celebrate. I mean, birthing is women's work, right?"

The bedroom door creaked open, and Grandma Louise stepped into the kitchen. Strands of gray hair had escaped her simple arrangement. Her eyes sparked in a way Zillia had only witnessed a few times, and knew shouldn't be taken lightly.

"Your thirst has cost you dearly, Jeb Bowen." Grandma Louise's Swedish accent grew heavier, as it always did with strong emotion. "While you drank the Devil's brew, your wife bled out her last hours. You could have spared a moment to bid her farewell. After all, she died to bring your child into the world."

Jeb stepped closer to Grandma Louise, and his lips twitched. Zillia knew he fought to hold back the spew of foul words she and her mother had been subjected to many times. Whether from shock or some distant respect for the elderly woman, he managed to keep silent while he pushed past Grandma Louise and into the bedroom.

Zillia stepped in behind him. Somehow, in the last quarter of an hour, Grandma Louise had managed to scrub away the worst of the blood and dispose of the stained sheets and petticoats. The blue quilt was smoothed over her mother's body, almost to her chin. Her hands where folded over her chest, like she always held them in church during prayer.

Tears threatened to spill out, but Zillia held them back. She wouldn't cry in front of Jeb.

The man reached over and touched Mama's cheek, smoothing a golden curl back into place above her forehead. "You was a good woman, Marjorie," he muttered.

"Jeb." Zillia stretched out her hand, but she didn't dare to touch him.

When he turned, his jaws were slack, and his eyes had lost their normal fire. "You stupid girl. Couldn't even save her."

Zillia flinched. A blow would have been better. *Surely the man isn't completely addled? Not even the doctor could have helped Mama.* She shrank back against the wall, and swallowed words dangerous to her own self.

Jeb stared at her for another moment, then bowed his head. "I guess that's that." He turned on his boot and walked out of the room.

Find out more about this book, and Angela Castillo's other writings, at http://angelacastillowrites.weebly.com

Made in the USA
Columbia, SC
01 April 2020